'Kirsty, can

Reid spread his h
this. Your eyes l
murder.'

Kirsty took a deep breath. She had been glaring. Her sense of humour suddenly bubbled unbidden from the depths, and before she could help herself she flung back a rejoinder.

'Not murder,' she corrected him. 'Castration will do nicely.'

His eyes widened. Then the wide mouth curved into a smile and the dark eyes twinkled. It was the first time Kirsty had seen the man smile and it sent exactly the same sensation through her as she had felt when he touched her. That smile. . . It was hypnotic.

Marion Lennox has had a variety of careers—
medical receptionist, computer programmer and
teacher. Married, with two young children, she
now lives in rural Victoria, Australia. Her wish
for an occupation which would allow her to remain
at home with her children and her dog led her
to begin writing, and she has now published a
number of medical romances.

Recent titles by the same author:

PRACTICE MAKES MARRIAGE
STORM HAVEN
ONE CARING HEART
LEGACY OF SHADOWS
A LOVING LEGACY

DOCTOR'S HONOUR

BY
MARION LENNOX

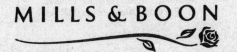

MILLS & BOON

DID YOU PURCHASE THIS BOOK WITHOUT A COVER?
If you did, you should be aware it is **stolen property** as it was
reported *unsold and destroyed* by a retailer. Neither the Author
nor the publisher has received any payment for this book.

All the characters in this book have no existence outside the imagination of the author, and have no relation whatsoever to anyone bearing
the same name or names. They are not even distantly inspired by any
individual known or unknown to the author, and all the incidents are
pure invention.

All rights reserved. The text of this publication or any part thereof
may not be reproduced or transmitted in any form or by any means,
electronic or mechanical, including photocopying, recording, storage
in an information retrieval system, or otherwise, without the written
permission of the publisher.

This book is sold subject to the condition that it shall not, by way
of trade or otherwise, be lent, resold, hired out or otherwise circulated
without the prior consent of the publisher in any form of binding or
cover other than that in which it is published and without a similar
condition including this condition being imposed on the subsequent
purchaser.

MILLS & BOON, the Rose Device and
LOVE ON CALL are trademarks of the publisher.
Harlequin Mills & Boon Limited,
Eton House, 18-24 Paradise Road, Richmond, Surrey TW9 1SR
This edition published by arrangement with Harlequin Enterprises B.V.

© Marion Lennox 1995

ISBN 0 263 79099 1

Set in Times 10 on 10½ pt. by
Rowland Phototypesetting Limited
Bury St Edmunds, Suffolk

03-9507-51360

Made and printed in Great Britain

CHAPTER ONE

'BOOLKURUNA. . .'

'You're mad.' The words of Kirsty's university friends still rang in her ears. 'To buy a practice in such a remote district as Boolkuruna. . . It has nothing but beach, bush and cows.'

'It has a town,' Kirsty had said defensively.

'Oh, yeah. Woongarra. Almost a city, for heaven's sake. How many people, Kirsty? Five hundred? Less, at a guess. You know what the Koori translation is? Boolkuruna means homesick—because it's so darned far from anywhere. And Woongarra means sleeping-place! You'll die of boredom in a week.'

'Want to bet?' Kirsty demanded of her absent friends. Excitement bubbled up deliciously. She was too young to be sole veterinarian in such a remote place—but the challenge was irresistible. And, even though she would miss her friends, relationships were something Kirsty wasn't very good at. Not any more. . .

'Oh, yes. . .' Kirsty's eyes followed the rolling hills inland, appreciating the wild beauty of the south-east tip of New South Wales. She had been driving through rain-forest for two hours, and was finally emerging to dairy country. Boolkuruna was cut off from the world. 'Yes,' Kirsty whispered again. 'I think. . .I think I can be happy here.'

And then her reverie was broken. Two hundred yards from the road a cow was lying motionless, alone in its paddock. Was it dead? Kirsty slowed the car to a crawl, and then pulled off the road as she saw what the problem was. The cow was calving, and even from this distance she could see it was in trouble.

It wasn't untended, though. As the sound of Kirsty's

5

motor died another took over. A tractor was coming slowly over the hill.

For a moment Kirsty hesitated, and then cut her motor completely and climbed from the car. Woongarra's elderly vet had retired three months ago. There was Kirsty or no one. She might as well start now.

By the time Kirsty reached the cow, the driver of the tractor had dismounted. She was a lean, grey-haired woman in her late sixties, her lined face grim. As Kirsty watched the woman lifted a pile of chains from the rear of the tractor and started carrying them towards the cow.

'Excuse me,' Kirsty called. 'What. . .what are you planning to do?'

The woman glanced up, surprised by Kirsty's presence. She'd been too intent on the cow to notice her arrival.

'I wouldn't watch if I were you,' the woman said flatly. And then she stared closer, taking in Kirsty's slim, diminutive form, the mass of black curls bouncing around the shoulders of Kirsty's red-checked sundress, and Kirsty's intense green eyes. She took a step back. 'Stephanie!'

Kirsty shook her head. 'No. My name is Kirsty Maine. I'm a vet.'

The woman didn't hear the last words. She narrowed her eyes against the setting sun. 'Dear heaven, you look so like. . .' She peered closer and then shook her head. 'No. I can see it now. You have freckles and she. . . You just look so like someone. . .'

The resemblance to the unknown Stephanie had clearly thrown her. Biting her lip, the woman turned back to the cow. 'Anyway, I'd leave if I were you. This isn't a normal calving.'

It certainly wasn't. Kirsty glanced down at the protruding calf. It had emerged backwards. Its hind feet were showing and it looked well and truly stuck. While she watched, there was another contraction. The cow rolled her eyes in agony, heaved uselessly and slumped back.

'I'm a vet,' Kirsty repeated softly. 'Please. . .I'd like to help.'

'A vet!' The woman looked up at Kirsty in disbelief. 'We don't have a vet in Woongarra.'

'You do,' Kirsty told her. 'As of now. What were you planning to do here?'

'I've tried everything,' the woman said wearily. 'I thought. . .I thought the only thing left was to attach the calf to the tractor and pull.'

Kirsty grimaced. She walked over to the rear of the cow and bent down over the protruding calf. Running her hands along the tiny legs she frowned, and her eyes widened.

'But. . . The calf's still alive,' she said gently.

'I know,' the woman groaned. 'But I'm going to lose them both if I don't do something.'

'Maybe not.' Kirsty looked up. 'I have my calving gear in the car. How far is it to your house?'

'Only a hundred yards. We're just over the rise.'

'Can you head back and bring as much warm soapy water as you can? Fast.'

'I can do that.' The woman fidgeted. 'Look, Miss. . .'

'Yes?' Kirsty was gently examining the cow. She wasn't too far gone. If they hurried. . .

'My father. . . This is my father's farm. He's old and he's a bit. . . Well, he won't spend money. He'd say. . . He'd say I shouldn't call a vet.'

Kirsty sat back and looked up at the woman's strained, haggard face. Some decisions were easy.

'But you didn't call a vet,' Kirsty said softly. 'I'm not officially working until Monday. As of now I'm still on holidays, and I don't earn money on holidays. It doesn't feel right. So let's get to work, shall we?'

The woman's unease deepened. 'My son. . . My son will pay you. I'm not accepting charity.'

'It's not charity,' Kirsty smiled. 'Your son owes me

nothing. I refuse to have my welcome to Woongarra marred by a dead cow. Please. . .'

The woman stood stock-still. 'You look so like Stephanie,' she whispered. 'But Stephanie never helped anyone in her life unless there was something in it for her.'

'Then be glad I'm not Stephanie,' Kirsty said bluntly. 'Now, if we're going to save this pair, we've work to do.'

What followed was a battle Kirsty had watched before but never participated in. The birth complication was unusual and usually fatal. The last time Kirsty had seen it, the vet she'd been accompanying had been called too late. They had saved the cow but had been forced to dismember the dead calf to deliver it.

Kirsty had been a student then. An observer. This time it was Kirsty doing the fighting—she and the cow.

Kirsty lubricated the birth canal as much as she could and started work. If she could pull this off. . .

It took time and sheer strength to push the calf back up the way it had come. It was impossibly, hopelessly stuck. The only chance for both calf and cow was to get it far enough back up the birth canal to turn it.

Luckily the cow's contractions were weakening. Each time the contractions came, Kirsty had to hold the calf in place, fighting the muscles which were moving to eject the little animal. The contractions gripped her arms like a vice, and it was all she could do not to cry out with pain. The last vet she'd seen do this had ended up white and shaken, and now she knew first-hand just why.

'Don't you dare move back,' she muttered fiercely to the now invisible calf. 'You stay where you are until I can turn you. . .'

And finally she did it. The calf slid another inch back—high enough for Kirsty to grasp the legs and turn it. It was the hardest physical effort she had ever made in her life—and the most satisfying.

She grunted in satisfaction as she felt the calf move slightly, and then slide slowly, slowly around to correct presentation. Mercifully the contractions eased for long enough to complete the manoeuvre.

Kneeling anxiously beside her, carefully pouring more of the warm soapy water down at regular intervals, the cow's owner was a picture of concern. She should give a running commentary, Kirsty thought, but she had no strength to do anything except hold the slippery body in place.

I must look gruesome, Kirsty reflected ruefully as she waited for the next contraction. She was lying flat on the grass, her slender arms elbow-deep in the cow. There was blood on her face and in her hair. But her fingers felt the calf move forward slightly and she forgot the damage to her appearance. She was winning.

The next contraction came and Kirsty felt the calf surge forward again, this time in the right direction. Her arm was crushed to the point where she wanted to sob with pain. As the contraction eased she finally, thankfully, withdrew her fingers. Now the calf was turned. It was up to the cow.

And nature took its course. Two minutes later, a fine heifer calf slid out to lie stunned on the blood-stained grass. It breathed by itself. Kirsty cleared the airways but there was no need.

Kirsty's bruised arms were forgotten. She knelt and checked the newborn calf, smiling with delight as the exhausted cow found strength to turn and lick her baby.

'I can't believe they've both made it,' she whispered to herself.

Then she looked ruefully down at her blood-smeared arms. And her dress. . . It had been red and white— now it was mostly red.

'Oh, my dear.' The woman knelt beside Kirsty and gently touched the calf. 'Oh, isn't she lovely. She'll make a fine wee milker.'

'She will that,' Kirsty smiled. She glanced over at

the pile of unused chains. 'Much better than the alternative. The cow would have died too, you know. The shock would have killed her.'

'I thought it probably would,' the woman admitted. 'But I couldn't bear to shoot her without trying. I'm so grateful. . . I don't know how you came to be here. It's some sort of miracle.'

'Pretty grubby miracle if you ask me,' Kirsty smiled. She looked down at herself and winced. To present herself to her prospective landlady looking like this could well be a disaster. She looked like an extra from the set of *The Texas Chainsaw Massacre*—after the chainsaw had been through. 'May I come up to the house to wash and change?'

The woman's face clouded over. 'Of course,' she said doubtfully. 'But. . .my father's up at the house. He's. . . He's not very well.'

Kirsty's smile faded. She looked down at the fast-drying blood over her clothes and then up to the woman. 'I really don't want to arrive in Woongarra like this,' she said apologetically. 'I won't disturb him more than I need to.'

'Of course.' The woman bit her lip. 'Of course you have to come. If only you didn't look so much like Stephanie.'

'Does Stephanie wear half an inch of placental matter from toes to eyebrows?' Kirsty demanded, and the woman smiled reluctantly.

'Stephanie would die rather,' she said softly. She shook her head. 'I'm sorry. Stephanie was my son's wife. We. . .we didn't get on.' She held out her hand. 'And I'm Margaret Haslett.'

Kirsty looked down at her gory hand and smiled. 'Do you really want to shake it?'

Instead of answering, the woman took Kirsty's hand in both of hers and squeezed tightly. 'I certainly do,' she said softly. 'Welcome to Woongarra, my dear. Now, come up to the house.'

The house was a shabby weatherboard farmhouse

set in a cluster of eucalypts. A flock of screeching
galahs were rioting in the high branches, almost drowning out the sound of the surf. From the front veranda
Kirsty looked down the valley to the sea. The view
was breathtaking.

'I lived here as a child and came back after my
husband died.' Margaret smiled, seeing Kirsty's
appreciative stare. 'My son thinks it would be more
sensible if we moved into town but. . . Well, it would
break Dad's heart.' She sighed. 'I love it here too.'

'I don't blame you,' Kirsty breathed. 'This is fan-
tastic.'

'Margaret? Is that you? Is there someone with you?'
It was a querulous voice from inside the house, and
Margaret took a deep breath.

'That's my father,' she said softly. 'You'll have to
meet him.'

She pulled open the screen door and went inside.
Reluctantly Kirsty followed.

The old man was sitting in an oversized rocking-
chair, just within the door. He started to say something
to his daughter as she opened the door, but as Kirsty
entered he broke off.

'Kirsty, this is my father, Les Hooper. Dad, this
is——'

Margaret's voice was urgent but the old man wasn't
listening. He was staring at Kirsty as though he had
seen a ghost.

'You!' he spat.

'Dad, this is Kirsty Maine.' It was a plea from the
woman. 'She's a vet. She's not Stephanie——'

'A vet!' The old man gasped and slumped back.
'Stephanie a vet! What bloody nonsense. . . What the
hell do you think you're doing here? Stephanie. . .'

'Hello,' Kirsty said uncertainly. And then, because
the old man was looking at her with hate in his eyes,
she put up a hand as if to deflect it. 'Mr Hooper, your
daughter's correct. I'm the new vet.'

Making what seemed a mighty effort the man pushed

his frail body from the chair. His eyes didn't leave her face as he took a wavering, threatening step towards her.

'A vet. . .' He shook his head angrily. 'Is this some crazy scheme to drag more money out of us? My grandson's given you ten times what you deserve, you scheming tart, and you're not going to get anything more out of us, do you hear? I'm still master in this house, no matter what lying tale you've conned Margaret with. You've had your pound of flesh—now get the hell out of here.'

'Mr Hooper, I don't——'

'I'm not paying, you hear me?' Kirsty had backed against the door but the old man was following her. His face was blue with effort and rage. 'Bloodsucker. . .'

'Dad, please. . .'

Margaret's voice was a feeble whisper, but suddenly a stronger voice cut across the room.

'Pa, for heaven's sake! What's going on here?'

The voice had cut across the room like a lash. Kirsty instinctively turned. A lean, wide-shouldered stranger was at the door opening into the back of the house. His tall frame filled the open door. Dark eyebrows snapped down over deep-set eyes narrowed in incredulity. His tanned, clean-shaven face was grim.

'Reid. . .' Margaret gave a small sob of thankfulness. 'Reid, your grandfather won't listen. He thinks. . . He thinks this is Stephanie but it's the vet. . .'

Reid Haslett's eyes swung to Kirsty. The incredulity deepened. 'My God,' he breathed.

'She's so like. . .' Margaret faltered. 'But Reid. . .'

'If she's not Stephanie then what the hell's she doing coming round at all hours demanding money?' Les Hooper interrupted. His rage hadn't abated one bit. His breathing was coming in short, rasping gasps and the colour was fading from his face. 'I'm not paying you one red cent, whoever you are. You can get back to where you came from, and if we never see you again it'll be too soon.'

'Dad, she hasn't——' Margaret crossed to clutch at her father's arm but as she did so the fight went from the old man. He stood stock-still, his hand came up to clutch the left side of his chest, and he crumpled where he stood.

'Dad!'

Margaret gave a sharp sob of fear but her son was before her. Reid moved like lightning. He was feeling frantically for the old man's pulse while ripping his grandfather's shirt from his chest. From the look on his face Kirsty knew there was no pulse.

'Mum, call the ambulance.' Swiftly he checked the airway and administered two sharp breaths. 'And you, whoever you are, if you're really a vet can you resuscitate?' Reid didn't look up at Kirsty. Already his hands were clenched together, pressing down in the first steps of cardio-pulmonary resuscitation.

'Yes.' Kirsty fell to the floor, realising automatically what was required of her. Without hesitation she moved to support the old man's jaw, pinched his nose and began rhythmically filling his lungs. She breathed again and again, willing herself to feel some response. Willing the old man to live. . . Breathe, wait, breathe. . .

'Is there anything you need?' Margaret Haslett faltered.

'The ambulance, Mum,' Reid repeated. 'Dial 000. Tell them I said it's priority one.'

Reid Haslett had obviously done some thorough first-aid training. The hands pressing down on his father's chest were skilled and sure, knowing just how much pressure to exert and where. Maybe he was a volunteer ambulance driver, Kirsty thought fleetingly, knowing that small rural communities often had to depend on such people. He was dressed as a farmer, in strong denim work-trousers and a faded checked shirt. His medical skills weren't those of a farmer, though.

Her mind twisted through this as she breathed,

pushing away the thought that with every useless breath her efforts were more and more likely to be in vain.

Nothing.

It was useless. Reid and Kirsty worked for fifteen minutes and in the end Reid sat back exhausted. His face was bleak. Kirsty breathed on. She wouldn't let go. . . She wouldn't. . .

Reid's hand touched Kirsty's shoulder in an unspoken command for her to cease breathing, and his dark face closed in pain.

'He's gone,' he said dully.

A strangled sob came from behind them, and Kirsty's efforts finally ceased. Reid was closing the old man's eyes as she rose stiffly to her feet. Kirsty's hands reached out to take Margaret's. In the distance a gradually increasing wail signalled the arrival of the ambulance.

'I'm so sorry,' Kirsty whispered.

'So you ought to be.'

Reid Haslett's voice was hard and cold as ice. He stood and came towards his mother. In a swift movement Kirsty was swung back, and Reid moved between Kirsty and the other woman in a gesture of protection. He took his mother in his arms and didn't look back at Kirsty.

'I suggest you get the hell out of here,' he said savagely. 'To come demanding money at this time of night. . . Even a fool could see how sick and old my grandfather was.'

'But I didn't. . .' Kirsty searched desperately for words but none came. 'I wouldn't. . .'

Reid didn't hear. His attention was only on the woman in his arms.

'It's too late to be sorry now,' he said bleakly, without looking around. 'You've killed my grandfather. Now, get the hell out of here. If I ever set eyes on you again I'll——'

His mother gave a rasping sob in his arms, cutting

through his words, and his hold tightened. Whatever his threat, Kirsty wasn't to hear it.

'Just go,' he managed.

Kirsty took a deep, ragged breath. What he was saying was so unfair—and yet this wasn't the time to defend herself. There was nothing else to do for these people but go.

She went.

CHAPTER TWO

KIRSTY had advertised for lodgings before she arrived, and the place sounding most suitable was a small farm a mile out of town. The woman who had replied to Kirsty's advertisement was a single mother—maybe not ideal, thought Kirsty, but better than living by herself.

Kirsty had said she'd be there by six o'clock. Her watch now said seven-thirty, and she still wasn't sure where to go.

Anthea Watts, her prospective landlady, had sent a map. It didn't help. Kirsty finished up at the bottom of a dead-end road, surrounded by bush and hopelessly lost.

Some vets would get right back in their cars and head back to the city after this start in a town, she thought desperately. Some vets. . .

An ancient truck was parked off the road, half hidden by scrub. As Kirsty sat and fretted over her map a man emerged from the bush.

Great. At least here was someone who might give her directions. Kirsty climbed from the car and called. The man, burly and middle-aged, looked up in the dying light, as though shocked to see her. He hesitated and Kirsty had the odd impression that he'd like to melt back into the bush.

So, to add to her woes, she was now just ever so slightly scared.

Slightly? She had to be kidding. Her knees had turned to jelly. Of all the stupid situations to get herself into.

'Please. . .' she faltered as the man silently stared. 'Could you help me? I think I'm lost.'

The man seemed to make up his mind. He dumped

what he had been carrying—a huge pile of nets by the look of it—into the back of the truck and crossed to Kirsty.

'I'm looking for a farmlet owned by Anthea Watts.' Kirsty was desperately trying to sound confident—as if she knew karate and judo and had a six-pack of automatic weapons right where she could reach them. It was just as well it was too dark for him to see the blood she was covered in. It might give him ideas.

Or it might make him as scared as she was.

The thought bubbled into her head and to her amazement she found herself smiling. To her relief the man smiled right back. Strangely, his smile also held a trace of relief.

'You're a bit off-course, love.'

Kirsty held out her map. 'Could you show me?'

And ten minutes later she was driving up her land-lady's access track.

It was a bedraggled and exhausted Kirsty who finally knocked on the farmhouse door. The woman who opened the door to her took an automatic step back-wards, and Kirsty didn't blame her. The blood and grime was still in place and she knew her face was as white as death.

Which pretty much summed up how Kirsty was feel-ing. Her feeling of responsibility for the old man's death was threatening to overwhelm her. It had been supplanted by her anxiety at getting herself lost, but now it crowded back in force.

She couldn't have foreseen what would happen, she told herself. But the thought wasn't comforting. All she wanted now was to crawl under some dark cover and cry.

Reid Haslett's furious eyes burned into her mind. She couldn't rid herself of the thought of his angry face—the pain of his loss etched into the anger. His words rang over and over in her ears. 'You've killed my grandfather. . .'

If she didn't pull herself together she was going to

have the door slammed in her face. Her potential land-lady was regarding her with real fear.

'I'm so sorry,' Kirsty said quickly as the door started to shut. 'But I'm Kirsty Maine, the new vet. I contacted you last week about a room. I. . .I had to deliver a calf just out of town, and then I went up to the house and the man there died of a heart attack and I'm filthy and. . .and. . .'

Her voice broke on a sob and to her horror she felt tears slip helplessly down her face. She put her suitcase down on the veranda and tried to wipe her face with her stained hand but the woman was before her.

Kirsty's new landlady was a woman not much older than Kirsty herself. She moved stiffly—her letter to Kirsty had said she suffered from rheumatoid arth-ritis—and her pleasant, open face was a mixture of concern and horror.

'Oh, my dear.' The fear had been supplanted in a flash by concern. The woman took Kirsty's arms and pulled her swiftly inside. 'Oh, my dear, I've been worried. I was expecting you by dinner-time and I was just telling Eve something must have happened. And look at you. Blood everywhere. You're not hurt? A calf, you say? And a heart attack? For heaven's sake, what a dreadful thing.'

Kirsty gave a strangled laugh. 'I didn't think. . .I didn't think you'd let me in the door looking like this.'

Despite the grime, Anthea Watts gave Kirsty a reassuring hug and pushed her back to hold her at arm's length. She smiled happily on her new lodger.

'I told Eve if we had a vet staying it might liven the house up a bit,' she smiled. 'And I was right. There's been more excitement in my house in the last two minutes than there's been for the last ten years. Welcome to Woongarra, Dr Maine. You're very wel-come—blood and all!'

Anthea Watts was a blessing. Her young daughter was a phantom-like presence as yet—a pair of huge eyes peering from around the door and disappearing just as quickly. 'She's shy,' her mother explained. 'We don't have many visitors.' She moved stiffly as she gestured up the stairs. 'I'm sorry. I can't help you with your luggage.'

'I don't need help,' Kirsty smiled. 'My parents trained me as a packhorse.' She followed Anthea up the stairs and stopped in delight at the bedroom door. The room was huge and spotlessly clean. It looked out over a rambling garden to open paddocks and, beyond them, the sea. She had her own bathroom, with vast white towels and sea-shells holding soap of every shape, size, colour and fragrance. This was clearly the best room in the house.

'This should be your room,' Kirsty said instinctively, and Anthea grimaced.

'It was,' she confessed. 'But I can't manage the stairs any more. That was a major reason I answered your advertisement, though. I couldn't bear to waste this room.'

And you needed the money, Kirsty thought to herself, noting the strain around the woman's face. This bedroom had the best furniture in the house, but it didn't need a degree in economics to look around the house and see that money was tight.

Her accommodation arrangement was going to work, Kirsty thought in satisfaction. Anthea seemed nice. Anthea seemed as if she could be a friend.

'There's dinner for you in the kitchen,' Anthea was saying. 'But it's already kept for an hour, so another half-hour won't hurt it.'

And Kirsty was left to stand under streaming, cool water and wash away the accumulated grime of the last few hours.

When she emerged she felt almost normal.

Almost. . .

'Les Hooper was old and ill,' she told herself aloud sternly. 'I have to stop blaming myself.

'You don't need to blame yourself, Kirsty Maine,'

she told her reflection in the mirror. 'Reid Haslett's doing a fine job of that without you.'

The memory of Reid Haslett's bitter eyes burned into her heart like a dagger.

Surely she'd feel better after a meal. Kirsty made her way down through the rambling house to the kitchen, where she found Anthea doing a crossword while she waited.

'I'll bet the wash felt good,' the woman smiled. 'I threw out your casserole. It was dry and disgusting. I've done you sausages and eggs instead.' She smiled at Kirsty, but as she looked her smile suddenly faded. 'But. . . But you look. . .'

'Familiar?' Kirsty grimaced, sitting down at the big wooden table. 'I resemble someone called Stephanie, I'm told. It's given me all sorts of trouble already.' And reluctantly, as she ate, she outlined the events of the afternoon for her shocked landlady.

'Good grief!' Anthea breathed as Kirsty's voice finally faded. 'Oh, for heaven's sake. You mean Les Hooper's dead?'

'Yes.'

Anthea sighed. 'Well, you can't be held responsible for that,' she said, unconsciously repeating Kirsty's conversation with herself. 'He's in his nineties, and he's had a bad heart for years. Margaret Haslett's lived with and looked after her father since her husband—Reid's father—died in a car accident twenty years ago. Les has been cantankerous, difficult, and in the last couple of years they tell me he's been quite strange.' She looked closer at the white-faced Kirsty. 'Not that I'm saying the resemblance wouldn't have upset him. But you couldn't have known that.'

'Stephanie is Reid Haslett's wife?'

'Was.' Anthea grimaced. 'But he's better off without her, if you ask me. Nasty, scheming little baggage, that's what I always thought. Though she was nice as pie to those who had what she wanted. And she wanted Reid Haslett as soon as he came back to town. Well, she married him, but she wasn't what you might call the devoted type. Took her marriage vows very liberally. Reid did a training stint down in the city for a couple of weeks and came back early to find Stephanie stretching her marriage vows so much he reckoned they'd snapped.'

Kirsty nodded. 'So he divorced her. And that's why Les Hooper hates her.'

'That's not quite all,' Anthea said savagely. 'Les Hooper had been worried about death duties on the farm. They've been abolished, but he was sure it was only a matter of time 'til they were brought back. Reid's his only grandson, so he deeded the whole farm over to Reid. When Stephanie divorced Reid she sued him for half the farm. And won.'

'Good grief,' Kirsty said blankly. 'I. . .I begin to see.'

'Yeah, and what I'm telling you wasn't the half of it,' Anthea added grimly. 'Reid had to sell some of the farm's best land and mortgage the rest to the hilt so his grandfather could stay. He's been working like a slave since then trying to pay off the debt. That girl. . .'

'Why on earth did he marry her in the first place?' Kirsty was trying to concentrate on pouring milk into a mug of coffee, but her thoughts were a million miles away. Or eight. Just about where Reid Haslett was.

'It's not hard to see that,' Anthea grimaced. Then she smiled. 'Try looking in the mirror some time. Now have you had enough to eat?'

'Plenty, thank you.' Kirsty rose and carried her plate to the sink. 'I'm. . .if you don't mind. . .I think I might go to bed now.'

'It's the best place for you,' Anthea agreed. 'You look exhausted. And heaven knows, you'll have heaps of work come Monday. After three months without a vet you'll have more ingrown toenails and desexing of kittens than you'll know what to do with. Reid Haslett'll be darned glad to see you. The locals have been calling on him to help with urgent cases, and he's overworked as it is.'

'Reid Haslett. . .?' Kirsty frowned. 'I thought he must have some sort of medical training by the way he tried to resuscitate his grandfather. Is he a vet?'

Anthea stared. 'Didn't he tell you?' she demanded.

'Tell me what?'

'Reid Haslett's no more a vet than I am,' Anthea told her. 'But he's a darn sight more competent in a medical emergency. Reid Haslett is the valley's only doctor.'

Doctor. . . Dr Reid Haslett. . .

It slowly started to make sense. Kirsty lay between cool sheets and thought through the events of the day. She remembered Reid's hands pressing rhythmically down on the frail old chest and nodded. He had to be.

Why hadn't he told her?

There hadn't been time. There had been time for nothing in the few minutes she had been with him but urgent medical team-work and then abuse.

She looked the spitting image of Reid Haslett's wife. And she had killed his grandfather. What a great way to meet someone she might have to work with.

Kirsty shook her head miserably into the night. Until Anthea had told her what he did, Kirsty had assumed she need never see Reid again.

'If I ever set eyes on you again I'll. . .' He hadn't finished the sentence. If he was the only doctor in this town, though, and she was the only vet, then they must meet.

Medical professionals in small communities were normally heavily dependent on each other. The elderly vet whose practice Kirsty was taking over had praised Reid Haslett's skills. 'The local doctor's a damned fine physician,' he had told her. 'And he's not above helping out if you need a hand with an anaesthetic at any stage. Mind, he'll probably expect the same of you.'

Not likely, Kirsty thought bitterly. Not now. Inexplicably, the thought made her feel totally depressed.

It should make you relieved, she told herself severely. He attacked you without knowing the facts. He attacked you without reason. He's a woman-hater, and he has reason to be. You assume professional courtesy if you meet him, Kirsty Maine, and that's all.

That's all. . .

She drifted off to sleep, but her sleep was troubled. The image of dark, angry eyes haunted her dreams.

The following day was Sunday. Kirsty intended to spend it getting to know the town and familiarising herself with her surgery. Woongarra had been told the vet would commence practice on Monday. Today was her last day of respite.

It really was a magic place. Woongarra township was situated at the mouth of a river, tucked into a cove where the cliffs formed a magnificent natural harbour. The waters here were sapphire-blue, both in the river and in the shallow waters of the cove.

After breakfast Kirsty wandered down to the beach, took one look at the beckoning sea and headed for the waves. This was part of the reason she had taken this job. Even in early spring, this district was warm enough for swimming. To have access to this beach. . .

She swam and swam, using the exercise to drive away the troubling events of the day before. The waters soothed and lulled her into peace.

Finally she emerged, sated with sun and surf, and as close to happy as she could get. Maybe yesterday hadn't been such a disaster. Maybe this job would be OK.

Glancing at her watch, she grimaced. Ten-thirty already, and she hadn't even visited her surgery.

Heaven knew what state it would be in, Kirsty

thought, as she walked up the headland from the beach to where the road from the town reached a dead end. She had seen the surgery the day the elderly vet had sold her the practice. It was a stark little building with one of the best views in the world.

'It's a hopeless place for a vet's surgery,' the old vet had growled. 'But I couldn't resist building here.'

Kirsty didn't blame him, she decided, as she let herself into the deserted building. She'd tied a sarong around her still wet bikini and her sandals were full of sand. Walking softly around the quiet surgery, with the huge plate glass windows letting in the vista of ocean in front and river behind, she started to feel sorry for every other vet in Australia. This was where she wanted to be.

A knock on the door startled her out of her pleasant reverie and she looked around. The door was open and a child of about ten or eleven years of age stood on the doorstep. In her hand she held a bird-cage.

Kirsty had hardly seen Anthea's daughter since she'd arrived, but she'd recognise those huge eyes anywhere.

'My mum says you're a vet,' the child said uncertainly. Her expression told Kirsty that with her bright sarong and sandy toes Kirsty didn't look anything of the sort.

'I'm really a vet,' Kirsty assured her. She smiled. 'I guess I don't look like it, but I am. And you're Eve.' She hesitated. Eve was clearly not paying a social visit. 'Can I help you?'

The child took a deep breath. 'My budgie's bleeding,' she quavered. 'And I know you don't start work until tomorrow, and Mum said he'd probably stop bleeding soon, and we can't afford a vet's bill but. . . . But I thought, seeing you were living at our place, I mean, it's sort of like family, isn't it? So I hoped. . .I hoped you might be here. . . His name's Custard. . .'

Kirsty tucked her damp curls back behind her ears

in a vain attempt to feel a bit more professional, and crossed to the little girl. She bent over the cage and her heart sank. A tiny yellow budgerigar drooped pathetically on his perch. Bright blood stained his lovely plumage and, while Kirsty watched, a couple more drops of blood fell to the floor of the cage. Not a lot of blood, but then this was a tiny bird. He couldn't keep bleeding at this rate and live much longer.

'Can you make the bleeding stop?' the child pleaded. 'Please. . .'

'Let's have a look,' Kirsty said gently. 'But first we'll have to close the surgery door. I'll leave the main door open to let the air in, but we'll close the screen door. We don't want him flying away on us.'

'He won't fly away,' Eve gulped. 'He flies all over the house and even outside, but he always comes back to me. He loves me.'

Kirsty swallowed. The difference between losing a cow a farmer valued at thousands of dollars and losing a child's beloved pet was somehow not equated at university. Valuable bloodstock was a veterinarian imperative. But budgerigars?

This little one was just as important as any pedigree bull, Kirsty thought fleetingly, as she captured the little bird in her hand and brought him out to examine him. The tiny heart fluttered against her hand and Kirsty grimaced. At her side, the child silently watched, the enormous eyes expecting the worst.

The bleeding was coming from the base of one wing. Kirsty's fingers gently parted the feathers, probing the soft flesh underneath. The problem was clear with her first touch.

'Eve, your budgie has a little growth at the base of his wing,' she told the child gently. 'It's been worrying him so he's started to peck at it. That's what's making it bleed.'

'Can you stop it?'

'Maybe. To solve the problem I need to put Custard to sleep and cut out the growth.'

'You can do that?' Eve asked, and Kirsty nodded.
'I can do that.'

The child nodded. 'You think. . .you think
he'll be OK?'

'How old is Custard?' Kirsty asked.

'Three years old.' The child shook her head. 'At
least, he won't be three 'til Friday week, but he
nearly is.'

Kirsty smiled. 'Well, we'll have to have him ready
for his birthday party.' Then her smile faded. 'I have
to tell you though, Eve, that any operation on a little
bird like Custard has risks. They can't stand much
shock or pain. He's young enough to come through it,
but there is a chance that we might be unlucky.'

'He might die?'

Kirsty nodded. 'He might die,' she said honestly.

'And if you don't operate?'

Kirsty looked down at the blood on her hand. 'If I
don't operate then he will die,' she said softly. 'I'm
sorry, Eve, but that's the way it is.'

Eve stood still, her eyes reflecting her dilemma.
Finally she took a deep breath. 'I want you to operate,'
she said slowly, 'the only trouble is. . .'

'Yes?'

'My mum. I mean, I thought if you just had
to put a bandage on she wouldn't mind, but if you
operate. . . She'll say we have to pay you and we
can't afford it.'

Kirsty nodded. If she removed a growth like this on
a large animal she would have to make a substantial
charge. This tiny bird would use anaesthetic—but con-
siderably more skill.

To do it for nothing, though. . . She grimaced ruefully to herself. Two procedures since she arrived and
she wasn't able to charge for either. And she'd been
in Anthea's house long enough to feel the woman's
sense of pride. She just knew Anthea would refuse a
free operation.

'Mum. . .Mum can't work,' Eve was saying. 'I. . .I

have five dollars, though. . . My grandma gave it to me for Christmas. But I guess that's not enough.'

Kirsty pursed her lips. 'How old are you, Eve?'

'Eleven.'

'What do you do with your Saturday mornings?'

Eve's fear-filled eyes widened. 'Nothing.'

Kirsty nodded. 'Well, you know I'm just starting as a vet. I've been thinking I could use an assistant. The cages where I keep animals overnight have to be scrubbed and my floors swept and washed. Would you be interested in such a job?'

'Would I?' The child's eyes lit. 'Oh, yes. But. . . How many weeks would I have to work for Custard?'

'Well, how about three Saturday mornings in return for Custard's operation and after-care? After that, if you'd still like the job, we'll negotiate a salary.'

'You mean. . .? You mean after that you'll pay me real money?'

'For real work,' Kirsty smiled. 'If it sounds OK I'll have a talk to your mum about it this week.' Then she looked down at the budgerigar. 'Now, let's get Custard more comfortable. Do you want to watch?'

Eve swallowed. 'I. . . If it wasn't Custard. . .' She had turned pale.

'I understand,' Kirsty smiled. 'Most vets have trouble operating on animals they love. Would you like to wait outside? It could take about fifteen minutes.' If it took any longer she'd have a dead bird on her hands. Because of the difficulty in breathing for such small birds, the only surgery possible was fast procedure.

'I'll wait.' Eve swallowed and disappeared gratefully out the door.

Kirsty was hardly dressed for surgery. There was a white coat hanging behind the door but Kirsty rejected it. If it had hung there for three months it would be less sterile than her inappropriate sarong. Swiftly she scrubbed down a small table and sterilised instruments. She had her own instruments in her car, but having walked up from the beach all she had was what the last vet had left her. He'd intended to stay until she arrived but ill-health had forced him to leave early.

She checked the drug cupboard and was relieved to find everything she needed right there. She'd rung the local pharmacy the week before she'd come and asked them to restock her essentials so she could start work immediately. The pharmacist had done his work well.

The anaesthetic was the tricky part. Birds this size needed so little and were so susceptible to overdose. Especially a bird that was already weak with blood-loss. . .

With the tiny unconscious body spread pathetically beneath her fingers, Kirsty started work. She had to be fast. Swiftly she cleared the feathers from the growth area. Her fingers gently probed the tumour. It didn't appear to be too deep. She wouldn't know for sure until she started cutting. If it went down too far. . .

It didn't. To her relief Kirsty found healthy tissue just below the surface. The tumour was a hard, well-defined lump, and Kirsty excised it with relief. If it had gone much further she would have had to leave part of it in place—with the risk of regrowth.

Now. . . She stitched with care—incredibly small, delicate stitches. Not for the first time she reflected on one of the few advantages of woman vets over their male counterparts. Kirsty had been taught delicate embroidery at school, and her stitching left her male colleagues for dead.

'Chain stitch or blanket stitch?' she enquired of the little bird, smiling. 'Hang in there, Custard. Nearly over.'

The operation was complete but the next few hours were crucial. Shock could still kill. Kirsty had turned on a heating-pad in her back room before she started. Now she carried the limp body in and laid Custard carefully on the warm surface.

She placed a bottomless cage over the pad, and put

a blanket over that. Warmth, darkness and quiet. There was nothing to do now but hope. Kirsty washed her hands, then walked out to the outside door.

'Eve,' she called. 'It's over——'

And she stopped. Beside Eve, Reid Haslett was sitting on the low stone fence.

CHAPTER THREE

As KIRSTY emerged, both Reid and Eve turned to face her.

Reid Haslett. The colour drained from Kirsty's face and she put a hand down on the doorknob, as if to steady herself. She had put away the memories of yesterday's events. Now they flooded back in force.

'Dr Maine,' Reid said slowly. His dark eyes were expressionless. He stood, the warm north wind whipping the light fabric of his short-sleeved linen shirt and light trousers. His deep black hair was tousled, as though he'd been running his hand through it, and the wind was ruffling it further. The man was almost impossibly good-looking. Kirsty's hold on the doorknob tightened.

She forced herself to look down at Eve. The child was watching her with huge, fear-filled eyes. At the sight of her, Kirsty pushed Reid's presence to the back of her mind and stopped swiftly to give Eve a hug.

'Custard's come through the operation brilliantly,' she told her. 'He's still fast asleep. Would you like to see him?'

The child nodded mutely. Kirsty took her hand and led her inside. Behind them, Reid Haslett was left to follow.

Custard lay still beneath their combined gaze. His wings were still spreadeagled. His tiny, blood-stained body looked impossibly pathetic. Eve's hold on Kirsty's hand tightened convulsively.

'He. . .he looks awful.'

'You would too if you'd just had a lump removed as big as his. To Custard, that tumour was as big as a tennis ball on a human. He's going to be pretty sore and sorry for himself when he wakes up.'

'Can I. . .? Can I take him home now?'

Kirsty shook her head. 'He's better off here on the heating-pad until he wakes—and he's better off dark and quiet. The jolting of the trip home is the last thing he needs just now. Does your mum have a car?'

Eve nodded.

'Then why not ask her to bring you here at about six tonight? Then, as long as Custard's OK, you can take him home in style. Would your mum do that?'

'I think so. . .' Then, more definitely as Eve thought things through, 'Yes.'

'There you go, then.' Kirsty led Eve to the door and gave her shoulders a reassuring squeeze. 'Now, off you go and enjoy the rest of your Sunday. I'll see you at six.'

Eve looked tremulously up at Kirsty, her eyes bright with unshed tears. 'OK, Doc,' she whispered. 'I'll see you then.' And she was off, her skinny legs flying down the headland.

'Which means you'll have Mum to bear the brunt of the grief if you end up with a dead bird at six o'clock,' Reid said drily.

Kirsty bit her lip. She was still staring down the road at the running child, her back turned to Reid.

'That's right,' she said slowly. 'And I can demand payment for the bill at the same time.'

She heard a sound which might have been a quick mutter of denial, but before she turned Reid had come up behind her. Strong hands gripped her shoulders, swinging her round to face him.

'I guess I deserved that,' he said bitterly.

Kirsty said nothing. Her eyes were watchful and wary. She brought her hands up to pull his arms from her, then backed a couple of paces.

'I'm sorry your grandfather died,' she said tonelessly. 'And I'm sorry that my presence contributed. . .'

'He was dying anyway.'

'That's not what you said last night.'

Reid put a hand to his face in a gesture of

exhaustion. The look made Kirsty's bitterness at her treatment fade. As his hand fell, and he looked as if he was searching for words, she shook her head.

'I am sorry,' she said gently. 'I shouldn't have said that. Your grandfather was dead and you thought I'd been badgering him for money. Maybe in your place I'd have been as angry as you.'

His eyes swung to hers. They widened in amazement, and he shook his head, as if in disgust.

'Hell,' he said savagely. 'It needed only this.'

'I. . .I don't understand.'

'That you're generous about it.' He slammed his hand down on the table and the sound made Kirsty jump.

'Please. . . You need to be quiet,' she managed. 'Custard. . .'

'Custard?'

'The budgie.'

'Oh, of course.' He laughed mirthlessly, and Kirsty cringed at the sound. 'Dr Maine's patient.' His words were mocking, as if she couldn't really be a vet.

Kirsty took a deep breath. She backed again to the door and pushed it wide.

'Dr Haslett, I don't know why you came,' she told him, 'but your presence here is doing neither of us any good. I'm sorry about your grandfather, but there's nothing more I can do. Maybe we need to talk professionally, but it can wait for a time when you're. . . When I'm more organised. Maybe at the moment your mother needs you more than I do.'

His eyes narrowed. 'Do I take that to mean I'm dismissed?'

'Yes.'

He didn't move. His eyes watched her—assessed her—following every contour of her slim body. Kirsty's unease deepened with every moment.

'You are so like my wife,' he said at last.

'So I'm told.' Anger was building within Kirsty's

head. She clenched her fingers into her palms and held, hard.

'I can't believe the resemblance.'

He stared for a moment longer and then, before Kirsty could make a move, Reid's hand lifted. It was as if it was drawn irresistibly to her. He ran his finger in a strong line down her cheek, down to the soft skin at her breast. As his hand reached the line of her bikini Kirsty finally reacted.

She gasped. She took a step back and struck his hand away. The sound of flesh against flesh reverberated in the small room.

'Don't you dare touch me!' The feel of his fingers had sent a weird sensation running through her body and she didn't like what she was feeling. She didn't like it one bit.

His eyes met her angry ones and his smile was apologetic. 'It's just——'

'Just that you can't believe I'm not Stephanie,' Kirsty spat. She was solidly angry now, her anger tinged with fear. 'But I'm not the unfortunate Stephanie. I don't have to put up with any more of your arrogant, sexist behaviour. This is my surgery, Dr Haslett, and I want you to leave. Now!'

'Or you'll throw me out?'

'Yes.' Kirsty crossed to the telephone and picked it up. 'Or the police can do that for me.' And then she bit her lip. The telephone was disconnected, of course. There was no reassuring dial tone coming through the receiver. She'd made an idle threat and she was on her own.

Then Reid had crossed to where she stood. With one hand he held her wrist, with the other he took the receiver and placed it carefully back on the cradle.

'Let me go!' Kirsty's cry was half order, half plea. She pulled back, but she was held in a grip of iron. 'Please. . . You're hurting me. . .'

He dropped her wrist as if it burned him. This time it was Reid who backed away.

Kirsty raised her wrist to her face and held it against her lips. It was a gesture of defence and of pain, and by the look in Reid's eyes it went through him like a knife.

'Stephanie. . .' he said blankly.

'No.' Somehow Kirsty remembered the injured bird and managed to keep her voice down. 'I've nothing to do with anyone called Stephanie, and if I hear her name again I'm going to scream, budgie or no budgie. Now, get out of my surgery, Reid Haslett. You've insulted me in every way possible. I'll try and remember you're suffering from the death of your grandfather, but all that means is that I won't lay charges for assault. It doesn't mean I have to be any more than professionally civil for the rest of my stay here in Woongarra. Now get out!'

To her fury, the pain and confusion in Reid's eyes slowly faded. Instead, the corners of his mouth twitched in something perilously close to a smile.

'I only held your wrist,' he said. 'It's hardly a capital offence.'

'You frightened me,' Kirsty said stiffly.

'I'm sorry.'

'I don't believe you.'

'It's true.' His voice had gentled, as if he were trying to calm a frightened child. He almost was, Kirsty thought bitterly. She felt absurdly young and absurdly vulnerable.

Reid held his hands up in a gesture of surrender. 'Look, Dr Maine. . . Kirsty. . .'

'Dr Maine will do fine.'

'Kirsty, can we start this again? I came here to apologise, and I'm damned if I'll meekly go home without doing just that.'

'So, say sorry and go.'

He spread his hands. 'I'm making a mess of this. Can you lower the fury-flags for two minutes and let me talk?'

'The fury-flags?'

'Your eyes look like you're contemplating murder.'

Kirsty took a deep breath. She had been glaring. Her sense of humour suddenly bubbled unbidden from the depths, and before she could help herself she flung back a rejoinder.

'Not murder,' she corrected him. 'Castration will do nicely.'

His eyes widened. Then the wide mouth curved into a smile and the dark eyes twinkled. It was the first time Kirsty had seen the man smile and it sent exactly the same sensation through her as she had felt when he touched her.

That smile. . . It was hypnotic. She felt like a small animal caught in bright headlights—held against her will. . .

'Maybe you and Stephanie have more in common than just looks.' He smiled, and then, at her look, he held up his hands again. 'Damn. I know you said you'd scream if I mentioned her. Think of Custard and don't.'

'I won't,' Kirsty said icily, but the laughter was still behind her voice. Her temper was failing her. Somehow she had to stay angry.

'Kirsty, what happened yesterday was a disaster.' Reid was speaking fast, as though he had to get it over with. 'My mother finally managed to tell me the full story last night, and I couldn't believe the way I'd treated you. My grandfather was in his nineties. He had terminal heart disease, and you walked right into a scene which was not your fault. After helping my mother you did your best to save my grandfather's life, and I treated you like a murderer. I would like to make amends.'

'There are no amends to be made,' Kirsty managed. 'I told you. . .I understand.'

'At least let me buy you lunch.'

'What, now?' she said blankly. 'You have to be kidding.'

'There's a great little café down on the foreshore. How about fish and chips on the beach?'

Kirsty stared up at him. 'Doesn't. . .? Doesn't your mother need you?'

Reid grimaced. 'My mother is surrounded by my three sisters, their attendant spouses and their various children. Most of them seem to be crying—including one of my brothers-in-law, who has drunk enough to be maudlin. If I know my mother, she has retired to her bedroom and locked the door. If I return home the various sisters and hangers-on will turn their attention to me.'

'So you ask me to lunch? How noble.' Once again Kirsty couldn't suppress a smile. Reid returned the smile in full.

'You agree, then?'

'No.'

His quick frown snapped down. 'You're still angry?'

'A bit,' Kirsty admitted. She rubbed her bruised wrist. 'But, on top of that, I can't leave Custard. He's still unconscious.'

'There's not a lot you can do if he takes a turn for the worse,' Reid said brutally. 'I've never seen anyone give cardio-pulmonary resuscitation to a budgie.'

'No. But if Eve comes back at six to find the surgery unattended and her bird's been dead for hours. . .' Kirsty shook her head. 'It won't hurt me to stay. I need to administer antibiotics as soon as he's alert enough to swallow.'

'What—no intravenous drip?' Reid's heart-stopping smile was back, and it was as much as Kirsty could do to keep her voice even.

'It's a bit tricky,' she admitted. 'Think of finding a vein in a premature baby, and then multiply the difficulty factor by about thirty.'

'So, no lunch. Isn't Anthea expecting you?'

Kirsty stared. 'How do you know where I'm staying?'

He grinned. 'This is Woongarra, Doctor. Everybody knows everything about everybody two hours before it happens in this place. By the time you open the surgery door tomorrow your reputation will have spread. You'll be known as the vet who tried to save old man Hooper, saved his precious cow and calf, and saved the Watts' budgie. Assuming the budgie makes it.' He hesitated. 'By the way, Eve told me how you'd arranged for her to pay. If you're serious about offering Eve a job—well, you couldn't have picked a better kid. Anthea is a real battler, coping with more than just her debilitating disease. She's living way below the breadline in order to keep her home. If you really intend paying Eve. . .'

'Of course I intend paying her.' Kirsty frowned. 'I don't make promises I can't keep.'

'No,' Reid said slowly. 'I guess you don't.' He hesitated. 'So, is Anthea expecting you for lunch?'

'No. I told her I'd find my own.'

'Well, then.' Reid gestured to an ancient Volvo parked in Kirsty's car-park. 'I'll find it for you. I'll collect some fish and chips and return. Don't go away, Dr Maine.'

'I can't,' Kirsty said crossly. 'But I don't think I want any lunch.'

'Then you'll have to sit and watch me eat it,' Reid told her smoothly. 'Because I certainly do.'

Reid returned twenty minutes later. By the time he arrived, Kirsty was thoroughly cross with herself. How on earth had she ever agreed to letting him buy her lunch?

She went in to check on her tiny patient. Standing there in the darkened room, she let her mind drift.

The sensations Reid had evoked frightened her half to death. She had sworn she would never feel that way again. No man would encroach on her carefully constructed, solitary existence.

'You know how you felt last time,' she whispered to herself. 'And Reid Haslett has the capacity to expose you again. So you can eat his fish and chips, be professionally aloof, disinterested and courteous, and then

you can assume a cool, professional relationship.
Nothing more.'

On his heating-pad the little bird blinked blearily
and Kirsty replaced the cover over the cage. She didn't
want a frightened bird trying to struggle upright before
he was ready. If he was left in the dark, completely
undisturbed for the next half-hour, Custard could gain
consciousness gradually.

So when Reid returned she had no reason to refuse
to join him.

Reid placed a huge parcel of fish and chips on the
grass. A vast gum tree removed the heat of the midday
sun, and beyond the headland the sea was a distant,
shimmering delight. This was the perfect place for a
picnic.

And it belongs to me, Kirsty thought suddenly, a
blast of happiness temporarily diverting her from
Reid's troubling presence. At least, it belongs to me
and my bank. The thought was almost too much for
her to take in.

She looked down and Reid was uncorking a bottle
of white wine. Two glasses were on the rug he'd spread
over the grass.

'You. . . You planned this,' she said accusingly.

He smiled. 'Forethought never got anyone into
trouble.'

'So you left home this morning thinking you'd wine
and dine the new vet?'

'Thinking I'd like to make amends for my treatment
of the new vet,' he said steadily. Reid rose with a glass
filled with ice-cold wine. He placed it into her hand.

It was a strange, dreamlike setting. This was her
new surgery. She should be professional—in control.
Instead, on her first day, she was standing dressed in
a scant bathing-costume and flimsy sarong, her feet on
soft grass and the surf sounding rhythmically in her
ears. And Reid Haslett was looking at her like. . .

She glanced down at her wine with fierce concentration. 'What. . .? What wine is this?'

'Rhine Riesling.' He smiled. 'An underrated wine.'

'I suppose that means you got it cheap,' she said sharply, and then winced at herself. She looked up, and to her relief found he was laughing.

'I guess I do,' he grinned. 'I know the local grower. Try it and tell me whether it tastes cheap.'

She tasted it and it didn't. Reid knelt and undid the newspaper parcel to reveal crisp golden slivers of fish, chips that were just right, and mouth-watering curls of calamari. He squeezed fresh lemon over the lot and looked up.

'Dinner is served, my lady.'

Something in the way he said it made Kirsty hesitate. She stood, glass in hand, looking down at him.

'You really don't want to be doing this, do you?' she asked softly.

His eyes narrowed. 'Would I be doing it if I didn't want to?'

Kirsty shrugged. 'You're under no obligation to me,' she told him. Nevertheless, she sat on the rug and picked up a piece of the fish. The swimming had made her hungry, and this was delicious.

They ate in silence. Reid's eyes stayed on her throughout, as though he couldn't make her out. Bother him, Kirsty thought crossly, steadily working her way through the chips. I'm darned if I'll let him spoil my lunch. She finished the chips and then eyed the last piece of calamari with longing.

'Don't mind me,' Reid said politely. 'You obviously have a bottomless pit in there.'

'Yep,' Kirsty agreed happily. She picked the calamari up, popped it into her mouth, and then rolled deliciously off the rug on to the grass. 'Yum.'

'You sound happy,' he said stiffly, and Kirsty closed her eyes.

'Don't you have nectar moments?' she asked. She was hardly talking to Reid. She was talking to herself. 'Moments you wish you could bottle and keep for always. I'm outside my own surgery on a day that can't get any better. I'm full up with scrumptious food and magnificent wine. I have a recovering Custard inside my surgery and tomorrow I'm about to start on the rest of my life. What more could a girl ask?'

'Is this all you want?' he asked, and Kirsty's eyes flew open.

'Isn't it enough?' she demanded.

He was looking at her strangely. It was as if he suspected her of putting on an act.

'When did you qualify?' he asked.

'Last April.'

'This year!' Reid shook his head. 'Mummy and Daddy are financing their little girl into business, then, are they?'

Kirsty's euphoria faded. Her face closed. Carefully she placed her wine-glass back on the rug and rose to her feet.

'What have I done to make you hate me?' she asked quietly.

'I don't hate you.'

'No?' She shrugged. 'You just enjoy putting the knife in at every possible moment. If you're trying to be friends, Dr Haslett, then you've a pretty funny way of showing it.'

'Your parents aren't financing you, then?'

'It's none of your business how I'm financing what I'm doing. Nothing I do is any of your damned business. Thank you for the lunch, Reid Haslett. I'm going in to do some work.'

'Your sarong is slipping.'

Kirsty looked down and flushed. The soft fabric of her sarong had caught when she stood. It had untied. One loop was still tucked into her bikini top but the other was hanging down. The tanned, smooth skin beneath her breasts was revealed.

Kirsty hauled the sarong up and shoved it into her bikini top, but her anger made her clumsy. Her fingers unloosed the other side and the whole garment drifted down. She made a grab but was too late.

'Let me.' Reid stepped forward and lifted the flimsy fabric from around her legs. Deftly he wrapped it around her, his strong lean fingers tucking it securely into place.

Kirsty burned crimson.

'You didn't have to do that,' she stammered. She took a step back. 'I don't want——'

'Me to touch you.' He nodded. 'I can see that. Now, what the hell is a beautiful woman like you doing burying herself in Boolkuruna?'

'I don't——'

'If Mummy and Daddy aren't paying, who the hell is? Have you been married, then, Kirsty?' Before she could stop him, Reid had reached forward and seized her left hand. He held it up to the light. A thin gold band lay on her ring finger.

'I see,' he said harshly.

'You don't see anything at all,' Kirsty snapped. 'Of all the arrogant, insensitive. . .'

'You mean, you're not like Stephanie?'

'No!' Kirsty pulled back from him, but her hand was held in a grip of iron. 'I don't even know your Stephanie. How on earth can I be like her?'

Reid didn't answer. His eyes narrowed to slits. Then, before she could make a sound, his hand pulled her forward. For a long, long moment he held her hard against him, her breast crushed against his chest. Then his hand came up to cup her chin, ruthlessly pushing her face up to his. His lips came down to hers, and he kissed her.

It was a cruel kiss. It was a kiss of punishment—a searching kiss, demanding questions that couldn't be answered. Kirsty held herself rigid in his arms, her body a mass of tense fury. How dared he. . .?

His mouth moved on hers, his tongue demanding an entry. He was bruising her, hurting her. Her hands shoved fiercely at his chest, but her strength was no match for his.

Dear God. . . Kirsty hadn't been touched by a man

for so long. She had sworn she never would be again, but she had no choice now. Reid's mouth was possessing her, wanting her, demanding a response. . .

And her traitorous body gave it to him. To her horror Kirsty felt her body give an involuntary shudder, and her bruised lips parted. She felt a tremor move through her—some instinct she had thought long-dead coming fiercely to life, like it or not.

No. . .

She heard herself whimper with despair. Her hands pushed desperately against the man holding her—and then the kiss changed.

Reid's hands dropped to his sides. She was no longer locked to him, but still the kiss lingered. It was up to her to pull away—to break the contact.

And she couldn't. Her face stayed lifted to his, as though she were connected to a lifeline. Warmth was flooding through her body. She could feel the forgotten stirring in her thighs. . .

Neil. . .

The name flashed through her head like a knife. This wasn't Neil she was kissing. This was Reid Haslett— a man who was kissing her because she looked like his wife.

Her lips closed and she pushed away. This time Reid didn't prevent her.

There was a long, long silence. Kirsty felt her breath coming in short, shallow gasps. Her sarong had slipped again. It lay limply at her feet, but she didn't notice. Her eyes were fixed on Reid, and her expression was one of terror.

What had she done? How on earth had her body been allowed so clearly to betray her?

Neil, her heart sobbed. But it wasn't Neil she was thinking of. She tried to resurrect Neil's face, but it was no longer there. There was only Reid Haslett, looking down at her as if he hated her.

'You'd. . . You'd better go,' she stammered. 'Please. . .'

'Kirsty. . .'

'No.' She gave a hard, bitter laugh. 'You weren't kissing Kirsty, were you?' she whispered. 'You were kissing Stephanie. I hate you, Reid Haslett. I hate you.'

He stared at her for a long moment. Then silently he stooped to gather the remains of their feast. He carried them over to the car, and then returned to where Kirsty stood. She hadn't moved.

'You don't, you know,' he said softly. He lifted his hand and touched her lightly on the cheek, and the touch went through her as if she were being burned. 'You don't hate me, Kirsty Maine. But as for me. . .'

He shook his head, as though clearing himself of a nightmare.

'I wish I could,' he said bleakly.

CHAPTER FOUR

HER wonderful day was in ruins. Kirsty mechanically checked on Custard, now sitting up on his heating-pad, and then attempted to settle to an afternoon going through her predecessor's files. It was work Kirsty would normally have found absorbing. As it was. . . As it was her hand kept moving to her mouth, remembering the feel of rough lips on hers.

Neil had never treated her like that. Neil never would have.

'Supercilious toad,' she muttered to herself. 'He thinks he can treat me any way he likes. Just because I look like his damned Stephanie. . .'

To her disgust she felt a tear of self-pity slip down her cheek. 'Neil,' she whispered, but she knew she wasn't even kidding herself. It wasn't Neil she was crying for.

Angrily she shoved the card she was reading back into the file. Her hand moved to take the next one, but then on impulse she skipped the rest of the 'A's and went to 'H'. There was no entry for R. Haslett, but a fat file on L. Hooper. Les Hooper. Reid's grandfather.

The story of Stephanie was clearly described in the files. Kirsty's predecessor had written himself a description of each farm when he had started practising twenty years before. Of the Hooper farm he had written:

> Fine dairy property. Three hundred acres. One hundred and sixty head, Friesian-jersey cross. Rotary dairy. Profitable farm.

There were the typical entries marked in the file associated with such farms. Routine testing. Mastitis. Accidents. Then, from four years ago, there was another terse entry:

Called to test and certify seventy head of cattle for sale. Farm divided. A hundred acres lost.

And underneath that, as though the elderly vet hadn't been able to contain himself, he'd written:

Damned woman.

Kirsty sat and stared at the card for a long time. There wasn't much sympathy for Stephanie in this community.

If Reid Haslett had walked all over his wife the way he had tried to walk all over her, then maybe she couldn't blame her, Kirsty thought bitterly, and then she thought of Margaret Haslett's weary face. Margaret had lost to Stephanie too—not just Reid and his grand-father.

A chirp brought her back to reality. Crossing to the back room, she found Custard had moved himself to his perch. Kirsty smiled down at the little bird in satisfaction. She'd adjusted the perch to an inch above the heating-pad, making it easy for Custard to reach and not dangerous if he fell.

'Well, at least one of us is feeling better.' She smiled, and then grimaced. She had been dreaming of this place for so long. Reid Haslett was not going to spoil it for her.

Not for anything.

Resolutely she turned back to the filing-cabinet and the 'A' section. Reid Haslett was of no interest to her. He wasn't interfering with her life any more. She had a practice to run.

She worked solidly through to six, when the sound of a car made her pause. Crossing to the door, she saw a battered Ford pull up in the car-park.

Eve Watts climbed eagerly from the car, but the child stopped dead when she saw Kirsty. Her face paled.

'He's not. . .? He's not. . .?' She couldn't make herself say it.

'Custard's fine,' Kirsty said swiftly. She tucked her sarong in self-consciously. This really wasn't the uniform of a working vet. Behind Eve, a tired-looking Anthea was emerging stiffly from the car.

Anthea's face forced itself into a smile as she saw Kirsty. 'Eve tells me you operated on our. . .on Custard. I. . . Look, we're really sorry, but if I'd known she intended. . . Kirsty, I can't. . .'

'Eve negotiated the account before I operated,' Kirsty said swiftly. 'Didn't she tell you?'

'She told me she's to spend Saturday mornings here. . .' The woman's face was still clouded. 'But we don't want charity. I'll pay. It. . . It'll just take time.'

'Anthea, I'm not offering charity.' Kirsty's voice gentled. She smiled ruefully down at herself. 'I know I don't look really professional at the moment, but what I'm offering Eve is a professional job. She looks old enough to scrub cages and sweep floors.' Kirsty smiled down at Eve's anxious face. 'Aren't you, Eve?'

'She's a good little worker,' her mother said doubtfully. 'But. . . But there'll be heaps of older kids who would love the job you're offering. And they might be more useful.'

Kirsty shook her head. 'I want someone who I know loves animals,' she said softly. 'I don't want someone cleaning my little hospital who ignores my patients. I want someone who won't feel silly chatting to a pet tortoise as they work. And I know Eve fits that description—don't you, Eve?'

Eve nodded seriously, but her mother's face twisted into the start of a smile. 'Well, she'll surely do that,' she agreed. 'Eve's the only person I know who holds conversations with snails rather than squashing them.'

Kirsty smiled back. Her instinct hadn't been at fault. 'Fine, then,' she nodded. 'The wage consists of all the vet-care Eve needs for her menagerie, plus twenty dollars a morning. That's renegotiable, depending on how much gets done. But I think you can earn that much, can't you, Eve?'

'Twenty dollars.' Eve's eyes lit up like stars. Her mother gasped.

'Oh, Dr Maine. . . She couldn't. . .'

'Don't you think your daughter's labour is worth twenty dollars a morning?' Eve asked.

Anthea stood back against the car. She looked down at her small daughter and a glimmer of pride sparkled under damp lashes.

'I guess she is,' she said slowly. 'And twenty dollars a week. . . Well, it would mean Eve could go to the pictures occasionally, and be like other kids.' She sighed. 'I don't. . . Well, you might have already guessed that things are as tight as can be. I trained horses and I can no longer do that. I've done a book-keeping course by correspondence, but there aren't any jobs in this town. Because of my disability I have to run a car, and there always seem to be expenses that I can't foresee.' She held out her hand. 'So, thank you, Dr Maine—Kirsty. Eve's job would be a god-send—and I'm sure Eve would love it.'

Kirsty smiled with relief. 'And I'll love having Eve,' she said solidly. 'Now, let's go and get Custard.'

Custard was still on his perch. Kirsty adjusted his own cage so the perch was near the floor, and then took the little bird from his heating-pad.

'Leave the perch down like that until tomorrow,' she told Eve. 'As soon as you get home cover his cage with a blanket until morning. You must keep him warm and out of draughts.' She turned and measured a small amount of antibiotic into a bottle, then handed Eve a syringe. 'He has to have this every morning. I can do it for you if you like, but I normally ask the patient's owner to do it. If your mum gives you a hand, do you think you can? Just hold Custard firmly, and when he squawks syringe it into his beak. Like this.'

She demonstrated while Eve watched, and Anthea nodded. 'We can do that.' She smiled. 'Though it seems an awful lot of trouble to go to for a bird.'

Kirsty looked up at her and smiled back. Anthea's eyes were a giveaway.

'Do you really mean that?' she asked, and Anthea laughed.

'I guess I don't.' She took her daughter's hand and squeezed. 'Custard's given us a lot of pleasure in his time. Though I wouldn't mind it if he improved his vocabulary.'

'Custard!' Kirsty grinned. 'You don't swear?'

'The last time I had an acute attack of rheumatoid arthritis, Eve moved Custard into my bedroom to keep me company.' Anthea smiled. 'I was feeling pretty rotten, and when Eve was at school I sometimes. . . Well, I sometimes told Custard how I was feeling. To my horror the crazy bird picked up exactly what I least wanted him to remember—and repeated my choicest words to Eve as soon as she came home from school.'

'Mum had to wash her mouth out with soap,' Eve grinned happily. 'But Custard still says them.'

Kirsty smiled down at the little bird and placed him carefully back in his cage. 'I'll take his stitches out in about a week,' she told Eve. 'And don't forget you start work for me next Saturday. Nine o'clock?'

'Oh, yes,' Eve breathed, and her mother laughed.

'She'll be here three hours early if I know Eve. Would you. . .?' She looked shyly across at Kirsty. 'Your car's not here. It's a long walk. Would you like a ride back home?'

Kirsty nodded thankfully. 'Yes, please.'

Anthea and Eve kept up a running commentary as Anthea drove. They were delighted to find Kirsty knew little of the town, so they detoured through the built-up areas, pointing out all the local landmarks as they went.

'This is our hospital,' Anthea said proudly. The car

had slowed before a large white building Kirsty had seen before. Like Kirsty's surgery, it was built high on a headland. Its view would be as magnificent as Kirsty's.

The building was fairly new, low-built, with wide verandas running the full length of the building and generous windows opening from every room. From the car Kirsty could see nearly all the windows were open, their curtains fluttering out in the sea air. A couple of patients were ensconced in easy-chairs in positions overlooking the sea.

'It looks a great place to recover,' Kirsty smiled, and Anthea nodded.

'It is that.' Her hands clenched tightly on the steering-wheel and Kirsty knew she was thinking of her illness. 'We're so grateful to Dr Haslett,' she said softly. 'He built this from scratch—put all his own money into it. Before it was built I had to go to Bega every time I was ill.'

'When your arthritis flared?'

'Yes.' Anthea sighed. 'Though it seems to have settled now, thank heaven. I haven't had an acute episode for two years.' She grimaced down at her hands, the telltale knobbling of swollen joints clear as she moved them on the steering-wheel. 'After every attack I'm just a little worse. Now, though. . . Now it seems Dr Haslett's almost got this dratted disease under control.'

'And you can start getting on with your life,' Kirsty said gently.

'No.' The hands clenched tighter. 'It's not as simple as that.' Anthea looked across at Kirsty, as though she was deciding whether to talk, and in the end the temptation to unburden herself was too much. 'My husband—Eve's dad—left five years ago. Before he did he ran our little farmlet into all sorts of debt. Now. . . Well, I'm so far behind in my payments that I'm going to have to sell. I can't get work here, and if I sell I'll have to move to the city.'

'No.' Eve's wail came from the back seat. 'No, Mum, we can't. What about Toby?'

'Toby's Eve's horse,' Anthea explained. 'Our last indulgence.' She sighed. 'I don't know. We could have fun in the city, sweetheart.' But by her voice Kirsty knew she didn't believe a word of it. 'And Dr Haslett says I can cope with administrative work.'

'Do you see a rheumatologist?' Kirsty asked, and Anthea shook her head.

'Dr Haslett's mum has arthritis and he's made it one of his specialities. He sent me to the city to see a rheumatologist once, but the specialist told me there was nothing he could do that Dr Haslett wasn't already doing. He's a fine doctor.'

'Reid came back here after he finished training?'

'He did his physician training first. There was an elderly GP practising here, but as soon as he retired Reid moved back. He's always supported the town. Even to the extent of marrying a local.' Anthea gave a small, mirthless laugh. 'Much good that did him.' Then she looked sideways at Kirsty. 'It must be strange for him—having you look like her.'

'He'll get over it,' Kirsty said wearily. She paused. 'Does Stephanie still live here?'

'Our Stephanie?' Once more Anthea laughed. 'Not on your life. I reckon she only latched on to Reid as an easy way to get out of this town. Then, when she realised he intended staying here, she took his money and moved on. Last I heard she was living with a theatrical agent in Sydney. That'd suit our Stephanie. I'll bet they have four bathrooms, a heated pool and a couple of maids.'

'He was a fool to marry her,' Kirsty said slowly, and Anthea shook her head.

'No. Not a fool. Blind, I guess, but then all men can be at times. Reid was young and overworked—I suspected he hardly had time for a normal courtship— and he was so busy he only saw what Stephanie wanted him to see. Stephanie was lovely and vivacious and laughing—she could make anyone laugh. She was kind to Reid's mother and grandpa while he was away. Nothing was too much trouble for our Stephanie. Until she had what she wanted.'

'But she didn't want Reid?'

'She wanted what he could give her. She wanted money and she wanted power. She left school early— she tried going to the city herself but found it an uncomfortable experience. This way. . . This way she was secure and cared for while she made her fortune.'

'I can't believe she was awarded half the farm,' Kirsty ventured. 'It seems so unfair.'

'I gather she copped a judge known for her feminist and socialist views.' Anthea grimaced. 'She reckoned it was unfair of Reid's grandfather to deed the farm over to Reid and deprive the government of its due. I think it was some sort of retaliation, but there was nothing Reid could do. Just pay and pay and pay. He's still paying.' She looked ruefully down at her car. 'The car he's driving is nearly as old as this. Another man might have just sold the farm and made his grandfather move into town. Not Reid. Not our Dr Haslett.'

'You really think a lot of him, don't you?'

'The whole town does,' Anthea said simply. 'I guess, in time, you will too.'

Some things just weren't possible.

Anthea's guesswork was doomed to failure, Kirsty thought bleakly as the car drew to a halt outside her farm. For her to think highly of Reid Haslett. . . Well, it would take little short of a miracle.

And his opinion of her?

Heaven knew what he thought. It didn't help matters one bit that the man couldn't look at her without seeing his wife. Kirsty put her hand on her nose and twitched it decisively. Maybe I'll have to have plastic surgery if I'm to live here, she thought ruefully as she smiled her thanks across to Anthea.

Nuts!

CHAPTER FIVE

MONDAY morning was chaos. For the first time since she had arrived, Kirsty didn't have time to think of Reid Haslett. Her small surgery was packed from the time she opened the door.

She had everything from bulldogs with weepy eyes to eggbound chooks. Many of the problems had been waiting since the last vet left, but there were enough crisis cases to make her realise her business was going to succeed.

She was going to need help. Kirsty hardly raised her eyes from the examining-table, and every time she did it was to answer the phone. She couldn't afford a veterinary nurse, she told herself helplessly. She just had to manage. On Monday night she did three calls out to local farms and fell into bed exhausted. When she turned up for work on Tuesday morning the queue was longer.

It inexplicably disappeared at about eleven. Kirsty saw her last patient to the door and looked in amazement at her empty waiting-room. When she had shown Mr Darby and his ancient cocker spaniel in there had been half a dozen people waiting. Now there were none.

'They'll have gone down to Les Hooper's funeral,' Ken Darby told her. 'I'm going there myself. The family are putting on a bite to eat in the hall afterwards but people will be back after that. They'll remember their place in the queue.'

'Les Hooper was popular, then?' Kirsty asked, and the man shook his head.

'Not much,' he told her. 'Tetchy old coot, if you ask me. Folks think a lot of his daughter, though, and the sun shines out of young Doc Haslett, as far as the town's concerned. They'll be going to show the family they care.'

He hurried off and Kirsty was left staring at her empty waiting-room.

She should catch up on some bookwork. Kirsty went to her desk and picked up a pen but her heart wasn't in it. Margaret Haslett's worn face kept appearing before her.

'They'll be going to show the family they care. . .'

Kirsty sighed. A funeral was the last thing she felt like attending, but maybe it had to be. She was part of this community now. Whether she meant to or not, she had hastened Les Hooper's death, and she cared for Margaret Haslett.

She removed her white coat, hung it on a peg, and ran a comb through her curls. She was wearing serviceable jeans and a crisp white blouse. There was no time to go home and change. This would have to do.

The funeral was in the cathedral—a vast stone structure set on a hill overlooking the town. The town fathers had assumed Woongarra would grow to be a city when they planned this building and it now looked faintly incongruous in such a rural setting. Incongruous but magnificent.

Despite its size, the church was close to full. Kirsty found a place at the back and sat quietly, letting the simple words of the service wash over her. She hadn't been to a funeral for two long years.

Neil. . .

Two years, and the memory was as alive as if it were yesterday. The pain. . . The awful, awful abyss of time between saying goodbye to Neil and the funeral three days later. Words just like this. . .

She sat and listened and the words blurred with memory. To her horror Kirsty found she was crying. Tears slipped soundlessly down her cheeks. She wiped them away with anger, but they were replaced with fresh ones just as quickly.

And then, blessedly, the funeral was over. The choir was singing, and Kirsty looked up to see Reid coming slowly up the aisle as chief coffin-bearer. His face was intent and solemn, but just for a moment his eyes lifted and met hers.

She saw him stiffen as he took in her reddened eyes—the crumpled tissue in her hand.

And then he passed, and his mother and sisters were walking slowly up the aisle behind the coffin. The people in the pew beside her rose to go and Kirsty rose with them.

Kirsty had thought she could slip away unnoticed. With the service over patients would return to the surgery and she had to be there. She needed cold water on her face and a few minutes to compose herself before that happened, but as she emerged from the cathedral she found it wasn't to be so easy. Margaret Haslett was standing with quiet dignity on the knave steps, her son beside her, greeting each person as they left the church.

She should have known. Kirsty paused in dismay, but she was being gently edged forward by those behind her. To escape from the line would be to draw attention to herself, and the last thing Kirsty wanted was attention. She bit her lip. There was nothing to do but go on.

And then Margaret Haslett was gripping her hand, her tired eyes looking with concern at the girl before her.

'Kirsty. . . Dr Maine. You shouldn't have come.' And then, as she saw the ravages on Kirsty's face, 'Oh, my dear. You are not to blame yourself. I won't have you blaming yourself. It was my father's time to die. Reid was upset when he shouted at you. He didn't understand. . . He didn't mean. . .'

Kirsty shook her head desperately. 'I. . .I know,' she managed. 'Reid came yesterday and apologised. It's not. . . It's just. . .I'm not good at funerals.'

Margaret's eyes fell instinctively to Kirsty's hand.

What she saw there made her draw in her breath, and Kirsty knew that she saw far more than her son had seen.

'Your husband?' she said gently.

Kirsty nodded. 'I guess I haven't become accustomed to funerals yet,' she said softly. She gripped Margaret's hands. 'All I came to say is that I care about you.'

Margaret looked at Kirsty's tense face and a weary smile lit her eyes. 'I believe that,' she said simply. Then she turned to touch her son's arm. Reid had been talking to the woman before Kirsty in the queue. He turned back to his mother, but when he saw who was beside her he stiffened.

'Reid, you know Dr Maine,' his mother said gently.

'I know Dr Maine.' Reid's eyes perused her face. 'Don't tell me. You always cry at funerals.'

'Reid!' his mother said sharply, but Kirsty smiled at her reassuringly.

'Your son hasn't a great opinion of me.' She pressed Margaret's hand again. 'It doesn't matter. Margaret, I have to go. I have patients waiting.'

'Then come to lunch with me.' Margaret's voice was suddenly urgent. 'Will you be able to come next Saturday? All my relations should be gone by then. Reid will collect you, won't you, Reid?'

Reid looked strangely down at his mother. 'You'll be exhausted by the weekend. . .'

His mother fixed him with a look. 'Reid, I really want to get to know Kirsty. Even if I am exhausted. Will you come, Kirsty?'

Margaret Haslett's eyes were pleading. In all of this, her eyes were saying, I need a friend. I see one in you. There was nothing for Kirsty to do but accept.

'I'll come,' Kirsty said.

Kirsty made her escape soon after. She was aware of Reid's eyes following her as she walked through the crowded church grounds.

The last thing he wants is for me to befriend his mother, Kirsty told herself grimly, but then remembered the pleading look in Margaret's eyes.

'So lump it, Reid Haslett,' she said out loud as she emerged out on to the street. 'Like it or lump it—so lump it.' She passed Reid's car parked on the kerb as she spoke. Angrily she banged her hand on the bonnet, and the car responded by starting to ring.

Kirsty stopped dead. For a moment she thought she had set off some sort of burglar alarm, but the noise wasn't loud enough. Kirsty stooped to look through the car window and the source of the noise was clear. A mobile phone was mounted on the dashboard.

Reid was the only doctor in the town. And someone was trying to reach him.

He'll be wearing a pager, Kirsty told herself. If whoever was ringing needed help urgently they'd ring the hospital and the hospital would page him.

And then Kirsty saw Reid's pager lying on the front seat of the car. For the short duration of the funeral he'd taken the pager off.

He wouldn't have had a choice, Kirsty thought sympathetically. To have his beeper go off as he carried his grandfather's coffin would be unthinkable. Still, someone was trying to contact him now.

She pushed down the knob of the car door, expecting it to be locked. The door swung open and a second later Kirsty was holding the mobile phone in her hand.

'Hello?'

'Oh, hi.' The voice sounded relieved. 'This is Sister Holland from the hospital. We need Dr Haslett.'

Kirsty frowned. From where she stood, she could see the undertaker closing the door of the hearse. The funeral procession was due to wend its way out to the cemetery for the actual burial. Margaret Haslett had need of her son.

'The funeral's not over,' she said shortly. 'Is it urgent? This is Dr Maine. . .'

'Doctor. . .' The woman on the other end of the phone breathed a sigh of relief. 'I didn't know. . .'

'I'm the vet.'

'Oh.' Disappointment.

'Can you tell me what the problem is?'

Vet or not, the nurse was glad to unburden herself. 'It's old Mr Freeman,' she told Kirsty. 'He had a hip replacement in the city a few weeks ago, and developed a blood clot in his leg at the weekend. Dr Haslett has him on a heparin drip, and the drip's packed up. It's been down for nearly an hour now and I daren't leave it any longer. I hoped. . .I hoped the service might be over.'

Kirsty grimaced. The nurse was right. After an hour it was urgent that the drip be restarted. If the clot moved to the lung. . . 'Isn't there anyone there who can reinsert a drip?' she asked.

'Sister Grey has intensive care training and can do it,' the nurse said. 'But she's on holidays this week. I'm in charge here and I daren't.'

'The orders are written up?' Kirsty asked.

'Yes. And the bottle's still nearly full. It's just a matter of finding the vein. But. . .'

'I'll come,' Kirsty said decisively. 'I can reinsert a drip easily enough.'

'But. . .'

'And I'll take responsibility.' Kirsty pre-empted the girl's next doubt. 'I'll be there in five minutes.'

It felt strange walking into the hospital. Kirsty felt a bit like an intruder on someone else's territory. The veterinary hospitals where she'd trained were just as clinically clean as this—but that was where the similarity ended. They didn't have bright curtains or big bowls of flowers and nurses in neat white dresses.

Some things were just the same, however. What needed to be done shouldn't stretch Kirsty's skill. The sister showed Kirsty where she could wash, and then led her through to Mr Freeman's ward.

'Are you sure about this?' the nurse whispered as

they walked through the long corridor. 'I mean. . . If you're really a vet. . . Maybe we should contact Dr Haslett.'

'The heparin's been stopped for an hour?' Kirsty demanded, and the girl nodded.

'And how long has he been on heparin?'

'Only since Saturday. He came in complaining of lower leg pain on Saturday morning.'

Three days. The clot would still be in situ. It could still be deadly. The heparin was vital to keep the blood from clotting further.

'It's been stopped for too long already, then. We either pull Dr Haslett from the graveside or I reinsert the drip. I've done this hundreds of times.'

'On humans?' the girl whispered.

'No,' Kirsty agreed. Then she smiled. 'But I spent part of my training at the zoo. I've put drips into lions, chimpanzees, a giraffe. . . The method's the same.' She grinned. 'Maybe we won't tell Mr Freeman what I've been practising on though.'

But Bert Freeman knew. His eyes narrowed as Kirsty came in. 'I know who you are!'

Kirsty smiled down at him. The man was in his seventies. He looked frail and rather scared, lying back against a mound of white pillows. Kirsty's patients never had it so good.

'You're the new vet,' he announced. 'My daughter told me you're the dead spit of Stephanie Trant— Stephanie Haslett—and hell, she was right. What are you doing here?'

'You need a new drip,' Kirsty told him. 'And Dr Haslett's burying his grandfather.' She looked down at the old man in the bed and smiled. 'He can't come and I'm capable of inserting a drip. Trust me?'

The old man stared up at her, his bushy eyebrows furrowed. 'A bloody vet,' he said slowly. 'What next? They shove bits of plastic in me leg and tell me I'll be right as rain, and then when I'm not they shove me back in hospital and tell me to lie still or I'll get bumped off by a blood clot—and now they send a bloody vet to look after me. I suppose you're going to treat me like a cow. I hope your fingernails are clean, girl. Next thing I know I'll be coming down with hoof-rot. A vet. . .'

'I promise I won't treat you like a cow,' Kirsty said steadily.

He stared up at her. 'How do I know that?'

Kirsty grinned. 'Well, if I was treating a cow with a gammy leg and a blood clot, I'd be seriously considering putting her out of her misery,' she retorted. 'I sure as heck wouldn't be putting her in a hospital bed with a drip.'

The old man cackled delightedly. He looked over to the nurse. 'You heard what she said. Don't you leave me alone with this woman.'

The nurse smiled, but she still looked worried. 'Dr Maine says she can reinsert your drip without worrying Dr Haslett. If you object, though. . .'

The old man looked again at Kirsty. 'I don't object,' he said slowly. 'Do your worst, girl.'

It was easier than Kirsty expected. Kirsty abandoned the arm the drip had come from, swabbed down the other arm and searched for a vein. Bert Freeman was wiry and lean, and his veins stood out like a road map. She slid the needle home easily, fixed it in position and then restarted the drip. The whole procedure took two minutes.

'How long before I start mooing?' Bert grinned, and Kirsty chuckled as she checked the flow rate against the written orders.

'About five minutes after the horns appear.'

She left him still chuckling.

'You'll let Dr Haslett know what I've done as soon as he's free?' she told the girl. She looked at her watch. Another half-hour should see the end of the official part of Reid's duties. 'I have to get back to my surgery.'

*   *   *

The afternoon was frantic. By the time Kirsty returned to the surgery all her previous patients were back, plus a few for good measure.

There were people here who had come out of little but curiosity, she thought wearily as the day dragged on. She was darned if she could find a thing wrong with Mrs Allan's Siamese cat, and Mrs Allan spent nearly twenty minutes grilling Kirsty on her background and intentions before Kirsty could finally close the door on her. And afterwards it was Mrs Frobisher and her Pekinese, and Mr Hammond's Labrador. Kirsty tried as hard as she could to be pleasant and forgive the constant questioning, but by the end of the day her temper was strained to the limit.

It was after seven by the time she finished. Anthea's dinner would be ruined again, she thought ruefully. She still had to finish her patients' cards and refile them. She might not be able to afford a veterinary nurse but she was going to have to get some help. And if the practice stayed this busy she could afford it. Wearily she sat down at the desk, her pile of patient cards in her hand, and then looked up as the door opened.

Reid Haslett. . .

And it wasn't a kind, smiling Reid Haslett either. It was Reid Haslett in a hell of a temper. He flung the door open and then stood glaring at her, his hand still clenched on the doorknob. Kirsty raised her eyebrows in what she hoped was polite, disinterested enquiry.

'Can I help you, Dr Haslett?'

For answer he walked forward and slammed his fist on to her desk. 'Do you realise what you've done?' he demanded. 'Bert Freeman. . .'

Kirsty rose, her heart staying where it was. Dear God. . .

'What's happened?' she asked quickly. 'Is he. . .? Have I. . .?'

'He's fine,' Reid snapped. 'No thanks to you.'

'I beg your pardon?' Kirsty took a deep breath. 'Did I do something wrong with the drip?'

'No.'

'Then, what the heck. . .?'

'Bert Freeman is my patient. I am a doctor and you are a vet, and I'll thank you to remember that. If anything had gone wrong with that drip. . .'

'Did it?' Kirsty asked, her heart rising back unsteadily into place. He'd frightened the life out of her, and she still felt shaky.

'No. But. . .'

'But what?' Relief made Kirsty angry. 'But you weren't available, so I fixed it,' she finished for him. 'So what's the problem?'

'You were a damned fool to do so. You left yourself—and me—open to all sorts of legal repercussions.'

'I see.' Kirsty nodded grimly. 'The great Dr Haslett's scared stiff of lawyers. So next time you see a dog bleeding to death on the side of the road you won't do anything because you're the doctor and I'm the vet?'

'That's not what I meant.'

Kirsty raised her eyebrows. 'Oh, really?' She walked to the door and held it wide. 'Dr Haslett, I really haven't time for abuse. I'm late for my dinner and I still have a mountain of filing to do. I reinserted the drip into Bert Freeman because I believed that no harm would come to him through my doing so, and that you were needed by your family. Now, if I've committed a crime, or done any damage. . .'

'Do you realise the legal implications. . .?'

'Bert Freeman's not likely to sue unless he grows horns.' Kirsty chuckled suddenly. 'And even then he'd reckon I warned him.'

'That's not the point. . .'

'Two points.'

Kirsty watched the man before her with interest. Would he hit her? He looked as if he was itching for just such an opportunity.

Kirsty caught herself. She was deliberately goading

this man. He had buried his grandfather today, she told herself severely. She was being unfair.

'Is that all you came to see me about?' she asked, her voice softening.

He wasn't to be placated. 'It's enough. You choose to practise medicine when you're not qualified. . .'

Kirsty shook her head. 'You're not really serious,' she told him. 'Reid Haslett, I chose to fix that drip because it seemed sensible and I was sure—not fairly sure—sure—that I could do it. It was well within my field of expertise and you know it. Sure, if things went horribly wrong the family could sue me. I weighed that risk when I decided to do it. On one side of the coin was pulling you from your grandfather's funeral. On the other was taking a very minor risk—not for the patient, but for me.'

'And I'm supposed to thank you.'

Kirsty sighed. 'It'd be nice,' she admitted. 'But I'm not expecting it. I don't think you can get far enough away from my resemblance to your ex-wife to treat me like a human being—much less a person with feelings that just might deserve some respect.'

There. She had said it. Kirsty fell silent and Reid didn't say a word.

The silence stretched on and on. She had only spoken the truth, Kirsty thought, but Reid didn't want to hear it.

'You really intend coming to lunch with my mother on Saturday?' he said at last.

Kirsty sighed. She went back to her desk and sat down. The man was acting as though he hated her. It just wasn't fair.

'Yes, I do,' she said quietly. 'I like and respect your mother and she wants me to come. So, if I were you, I'd find another engagement on Saturday afternoon.'

'You didn't seriously think I'd come too?'

Kirsty's green eyes flashed fury. Of all the arrogant. . . 'No,' she snapped. 'I didn't. At least, I hoped like hell that you wouldn't. Because you are a

rude, overbearing, arrogant pig, Reid Haslett. You are
not welcome in this surgery. This place is a place for
sick animals, and I'd rather have a leprous goat in here
than you.'

'A leprous goat. . .'

Reid repeated the words blankly. He stood looking
down at her, and then the corners of his mouth twisted
into a reluctant smile. 'I don't think there is such
a thing.'

'You'd know,' Kirsty said sarcastically. 'You're the
doctor.'

'Kirsty. . .'

'Yes?' Kirsty raised her eyebrows in what she desperately hoped was cool enquiry. Inside she was a
trembling jelly, but somehow she had to retain her
composure.

'Let me help you with the filing.'

Kirsty took a deep breath. 'Go jump, Dr Haslett,'
she said distinctly, 'off something very high, and prefer-
ably into something very hard.' She picked up a pen
and started writing. Go away, her tired mind pleaded.
Just get the heck out of there.

He turned and the door opened. Thank goodness for
that, Kirsty thought thankfully, but then thought again.

'Dr Maine?'

It wasn't Reid Haslett going out. It was Eve Watts
coming in.

Kirsty looked up swiftly. The child was standing
at the door, clutching the knob as though her
life depended on it. Her breath was coming in
frightened gasps.

'Oh, my dear,' Kirsty said, rising. 'Is it Custard?'

'No.' Eve swallowed. 'Nothing's wrong with
Custard,' she said desperately. 'It's just. . .I
thought. . .I wondered if. . .I wondered if you might
be coming home soon.'

Kirsty's eyes widened. The child had just run over
a mile in the near dark—to see if she 'might be coming
home soon'?

'Hey, Eve.' Reid's hand came down on the child's shoulder and he spoke in a tone Kirsty hardly recognised. 'What's the problem with your mum?'

He had gone straight to the heart of the matter, it seemed. Eve raised tear-filled eyes to his and there was relief in her face.

'I'm not supposed to tell you. . .'

'Tell Kirsty, then. Don't tell me.'

Eve nodded, the relief still there. It seemed that though she'd been forbidden to tell Reid, that was exactly what she wanted to do. This way she could tell him indirectly. She turned back to Kirsty, but half an eye was still on Reid.

'I came home from school and Mum was crying,' Eve stammered to Kirsty. 'Her leg's sore. Her knee. . . It's not just that, though. She said. . . She said that she's had a letter from the bank. She says we're going to have to sell the farm. Mum asked the bank for time now that we have a lodger—but the bank says it's not enough money coming in to pay all the debts. And then Mum was carrying sandwiches to the table and she fell over because her knee was hurting her so much. And she's hurt it more. And she's lying on the floor crying. And I wanted to call Dr Haslett because her knee looks all red and swollen but she said, "Don't you dare," and she says Dr Haslett never charges full rate and she's damned if she's accepting any more charity. . . And she said she'd cut the damned thing off, it hurt so much. . .' Eve's small face crumpled and she faltered. 'And I just wanted to know if you were coming home.'

It was an outright plea.

'Of course I'll come,' Kirsty told her, but Reid shook his head.

'Not yet,' he told her. His grip on Eve tightened. 'I'll go by myself.'

'But she said——' Eve started.

'She said you weren't to tell me. Well, you didn't tell me. You told Dr Maine, not me. Now, I've just read of a new drug they're trialling for your mum's arthritis. I might pop in and see her this very night, and if you and Kirsty arrived home ten minutes later—well, that'd be just chance, wouldn't it?'

Eve's face cleared. 'You'd do that. . .'

'I'm going now.' Reid glanced up at Kirsty. 'How about finding young Eve a floor to sweep, Dr Maine?' His eyes were giving her a silent message. Ten minutes in case things were bad. Maybe a little more. . .

Kirsty nodded briefly. Message understood.

And he was gone.

Kirsty found a more satisfactory job than sweeping for the distraught Eve. In the back room she had a pup who'd come in looking as if he was heading for distemper. Half an hour after the pup's owner had tearfully agreed to let Kirsty keep him overnight to watch, the pup had decided to make a miraculous recovery. He now greeted Eve with delight, licking the little girl's tearstained face and turning her gulping sobs to chuckles.

'That's just what he needed,' Kirsty told Eve fifteen minutes later, replacing the squirming pup in his cage. 'Sometimes I think a good cuddle works better than antibiotics.'

'Truly?' Kirsty grimaced into the dark. For people too. . .

If Anthea had to sell the farm, Kirsty would have to move on. She'd miss them. . .

What a selfish thought, Kirsty told herself crossly as she drove down the headland. It was just that it seemed so good—and if she left Anthea's farm she might be forced to live alone. . .

Alone. . .

The thought flashed through her in a desolate wave and she clenched her fingers around the steering-wheel. Heavens, she should be used to it by now.

There must be a way for Anthea to keep her little farm. . .

As she pulled the car to a halt, Kirsty thought that

Anthea's home was worth fighting for. It was too big for three people and one horse, though. There were horse-yards round the house and stables—by the look of it housing for thirty or more horses. And the only horse they had was Eve's Toby.

Reid's car wasn't outside. . .

'Maybe he didn't come,' Eve said tentatively as they pulled to a halt. Her voice was full of dread.

'He came. Dr Haslett wouldn't break a promise.' Kirsty knew it was true.

'So where is he?' Eve had hauled open the car door and was running towards the house. 'Mum. . .'

The house was empty. Kirsty walked through to the kitchen. Nothing. . .

For a moment she felt sick. Supposing he hadn't come. Supposing Anthea had done something stupid. . . And then, even as she turned to face Eve's terror, the phone began to ring.

'Dr Maine?' It was an efficient woman's voice.

'Yes.'

'Dr Haslett said to let you know he brought Mrs Watts straight in to Casualty. If you could bring her daughter down. . .'

'Anthea's OK?' It was hard to keep the anxiety from her voice when Eve's enormous eyes were watching for any trace of fear.

'She's as well as can be expected. . .'

'Don't give me that,' Kirsty snapped. The standard answer. The hospital had told her that when she'd had to ring about Neil, and it made her feel sick. 'I have her daughter here. Why did Dr Haslett take her to hospital?'

'Dr Haslett will talk to you when——'

'By the time I get to the hospital the child will have panicked herself to illness.' Kirsty cut across the efficient, unemotional tones. 'And I'll hold you responsible. Tell me what's going on. Now!'

It worked. Nothing like holding someone personally responsible. The woman on the other end of the line hesitated, and thought better of her intransigence.

'Mrs Watts' knee is very swollen,' the nurse admitted reluctantly. 'Dr Haslett's concerned that it may be septic arthritis. . .'

Septic arthritis. . . Bad enough, but not a frightening diagnosis to throw at Eve. Much better than the things Eve's young face showed she was dreading.

'We'll come straight down,' Kirsty told the nurse, and put the phone down. Then she crossed swiftly to give Eve a reassuring hug.

'It's OK. Your mum didn't do anything silly. I guess you knew she wouldn't. Dr Haslett's taken her to hospital because he's worried her knee has an infection in it.'

'Is that all?' Eve stared up, plainly at a loss to understand why Reid would have taken her so quickly.

It wasn't quite all, Kirsty knew. If the knee was septic then the consequences could be disastrous. Anthea had threatened to cut off her leg. A septic knee could mean that it had to be done anyway. The consequences of missed septicaemia could even be tragic.

'If it's septic arthritis then Dr Haslett will be in a hurry to start antibiotics,' Kirsty told her. 'The quicker the infection's brought under control the less damage there'll be to the knee. Now, let's pack a nightgown and toothbrush for your mum, and go down and see her.'

Reid Haslett met them as they entered Casualty. Kirsty hadn't seen him in white coat with stethoscope attached before. He looked different—a professional she could almost relate to.

'Hi, Eve.' Reid came across to where they were standing. 'We've just sent your mum up to the ward. You can go through and see her if you like. Room Twelve.'

Eve stared straight at him. 'What's the matter with her?' She had obviously meant it to sound casual, but the words sounded belligerent and scared stiff. 'Why are you putting her in hospital?'

Reid looked down at the vial of straw-coloured fluid he was holding in his hand. Then, as if making a decision, he motioned Eve to a chair. 'Sit down, Eve.' And he sat himself on the other side of the desk.

Kirsty watched in admiration. His tactics were to speak to Eve as a caring, adult relative. A little of the belligerence faded from Eve's face but the fear was still there.

'Your mum's knee was swollen,' Reid told Eve. 'You could see that, and you were quite right to be worried. Sometimes with rheumatoid arthritis the joints can become septic. Infected. It's rare but it happens, and when it happens it can cause major problems very fast.'

'And that happened to Mum?'

'I don't think so.' Reid motioned to the vial he was still holding. 'I brought your mum down in a hurry because I thought things might have been worse than they were. When she fell at teatime she bruised her knee and that made the swelling worse—it made the chance of septic arthritis seem more likely. When I got her here, though, I put some local anaesthetic into her knee and aspirated—sucked out through a syringe—some fluid.' He held it up to the light. 'From here it looks good. The colour's normal. I'm going to check it now under the microscope to see if we have any bacteria present.' He hesitated again. 'Want to watch?'

Eve nodded soundlessly and rose. Reid held out his hand. 'Coming too, Dr Maine?'

Kirsty shook her head. Reid was coping just fine with the frightened child. 'I'll go talk to Anthea,' she smiled.

Room Twelve was right next door to Mr Freeman's. On impulse Kirsty put her head round the door as she passed. Bert Freeman was watching a small television on a swinging stand. He turned as she entered and his face creased in delight when he saw who it was.

'Going fine,' he told her, lifting his arm with drip attached. 'Doc Haslett checked it and couldn't find a darn thing wrong with it.' He paused. 'Seemed a mite put out, though.'

'I guess he thought I was trying to put him out of a job.'

'You're here to treat someone else, then?' Bert demanded, and Kirsty shook her head.

'Just thought I'd drop in and see how the horns are progressing,' she teased, and the elderly man grinned.

'Moo!' he called. Kirsty chatted with him for a couple of moments and retreated, laughing. No legal implications there, it seemed.

Anthea was lying white-faced and anxious in the next ward. She raised herself awkwardly on the pillows as Kirsty entered.

'Kirsty. . . Did you bring Eve?'

'I did. She's with Dr Haslett, looking down a microscope at your knee fluid,' Kirsty told her, and then looked behind. Doctor and child were walking down the corridor. The fear had lifted from Eve's face.

'Mum, it's OK.' The child launched herself at her mother's bed. 'Dr Haslett says he can't see a single bacteria—I mean bacterium, because he says that's what one is, and he can't see even one bacterium—and there's probably nothing wrong with your knee except a bit more of your ordinary arthritis and then bruises from where you fell. He says he'll send the fluid off to the lab to make sure, and you have to stay here for two days to rest, but you won't have to chop your leg off after all.'

Anthea hugged her daughter hard. When she emerged from the embrace her face was wet. She gave a half-hearted chuckle. 'As if I would. . . Oh, Eve, I'm sorry for frightening you, honey. Mummy was being stupid.'

'It's OK.' Resolution was written on Eve's face. 'As long as you keep your leg it'll be OK. Even moving from the farm. . .'

'Maybe it will.' Anthea took a deep breath. 'And we might not have to go to the city. There are twenty acres at home that aren't being used, and Toby can do with less. If we sell, I could maybe rent a house with a paddock for Toby. And maybe——' Anthea cast a scared glance up at Reid, as though she didn't quite believe what he had been saying '—maybe Dr Haslett knows an agency that can find Daddy. He thinks Daddy should be helping pay for you. If he did—then maybe we could stay in Woongarra.'

Kirsty glanced over at Reid. He was watching calmly, and her opinion of him went up a notch. Even if nothing came of this—if Eve's father couldn't be located—the thought of possible financial help might get Anthea through the darkness of tonight.

'But if you get sick again. . .' Eve said.

'There's a strong possibility that your mum won't,' Reid told Eve firmly. 'Rheumatoid arthritis is more fickle than your Toby. It kicks you just like Toby did the first day you got him, and then it can be nice as pie for ever and ever.'

'Toby's kicked me four times,' Eve said doubtfully.

'And will he kick you again?' Reid smiled.

'He'd better not!'

'There you are, then.' Reid rumpled Eve's hair. 'We're saying exactly the same of your mum's disease. It kicked her tonight, but not too hard. It was just the culmination of a bad day and the fall which made it seem so bad. And there's a new drug being trialled at the moment which is promising wonders. This is a small flare-up, Anthea.'

'I know.' Anthea managed a watery smile. 'I'm sorry. It's just. . .I get so bored sitting at home day after day. And then a letter like the one from the bank comes and I've nothing to do but think about it. It might be worth going to the city just to get me employed. Otherwise I'm going to be an introverted depressive by the time I'm forty.' She glared down at her swollen fingers, as though she hated them. 'All I know is horses. But maybe something like the Citizens' Advice Bureau. . .or reading to the patients in hospital. . .'

'It's better than sitting at home feeling sorry for yourself,' Reid said brutally. 'And I'm darned if I'm prescribing antidepressants yet. You're too young to be consigning the rest of your life to the "useless and dependent" basket.'

'It seems that's all I've been doing.' Anthea looked at Kirsty. 'I'm sorry, Kirsty. I didn't even make you dinner. I've rung my mother—Eve's grandmother. She'll pick Eve up here and stay at the farm while I'm in hospital. I'm sure she won't mind making you something. . .'

'I'm perfectly capable of cooking my own dinner later,' Kirsty assured her. 'And I can look after Eve.' It wasn't the only way she could help. Her mind was racing as she talked.

'Not if you get called out at night,' Reid said firmly. 'Grandma it is, young Eve.'

'Anthea, how disabled are you?' Kirsty asked suddenly.

Reid flashed her a look, as though expecting some cruel remark to come next. Resolutely Kirsty kept her eyes on Eve's mother.

'I can't do anything I used to do,' Anthea told her. 'My joints are stiff. I can't walk very far or do fiddly things with my fingers. I can't sew.' She shrugged. 'I can do bookwork and answer telephones, so there might be something. . .'

'Could you do full-time receptionist work?'

Reid's eyes flew wide. He started to say something but then thought better of it. Quietly his hand lifted on the bedside table, then he let it fall again, his fingers drumming a silent rhythm.

'I can't type. And I can't sit still or stand for very long. Half an hour without stretching and I start to stiffen.'

Kirsty nodded. 'But within those limitations you can work?'

'I guess. . .I guess so.'

'Then would you like a job as my receptionist?'

'Would I. . .?' Anthea stared. Then she shook her head. 'But you don't need a receptionist.'

'Don't I just?' Kirsty said grimly. 'I've had two days of hell. I thought this would be a quiet little practice where I could act as my own receptionist. I'm way behind already.'

'What. . .what would I have to do?'

'Everything.' Kirsty grinned. 'Answer the phone that never stops ringing and do all my scheduling of appointments and farm-calls. Keep the patients from each other's throats while they wait. This afternoon I had two Dobermanns in the waiting-room with one pathetic kitten. The Dobermann owner was worse than useless. I ended up having to treat the dogs before their turn just to get rid of them. My receptionist would sort problems like that out—if necessary insisting that one or the other wait outside—and then stay on hand to ensure they did it. I'd also call on you to give me a hand in surgery sometimes. And, if you were agreeable, I'd put your phone number on my card as a back-up. If I could use you as back-up I wouldn't have to depend entirely on a mobile phone—something which is the pits when I'm trying to do a difficult procedure. I'd let you know where to find me in emergencies.'

Anthea's eyes were almost sparkling. 'I could do that,' she said softly. 'But. . . But I can't type.'

'Unlike my colleague here——' Kirsty flashed a malicious look at Reid as she spoke '——I hardly ever refer my patients to specialists. There's very little typing, and what there is I can do myself.'

Anthea stiffened. 'You mean you're just giving me the job to be kind. You'll have to do some of my work for me.'

Kirsty sighed. 'I'm not,' she said definitely. 'I know

I can get a sixteen-year-old receptionist who can type.
I don't know that she'll be dependable. She won't be
able to answer my calls out of hours. She won't be able
to sort serious calls from nonsense. The farmers won't
respect her—they'll insist on talking direct to me. I
mightn't like her, and her daughter won't brighten up
my surgery. I'd like you for the job, Anthea Watts.
Do you want it?'

'Oh, Mum. . .'

Anthea looked at Kirsty for a long moment. Her
eyes then fell to her daughter, across to Reid, and
then finally back to Kirsty. Finally she began to smile.
'If I could find a job maybe the bank would give me
more time—and even if they didn't and I had to sell
then I could still live at Woongarra. . .'

'You mean you're interested?' Kirsty smiled.

'When would you like me to start?'

'How about as soon as your knee will take it?' Kirsty
said promptly, and Anthea's smile broadened.

'Really?'

'Really. Please say yes.'

'Yes, please,' Anthea said.

Reid left two minutes later. As he left he gripped
Anthea's hand and smiled down at her.

'Better than an antidepressant?' he asked, and
Anthea laughed. She sounded suddenly young.

'Much better.'

His gaze swung around to Kirsty. 'I need to talk to
you, Dr Maine,' he told her. 'Now, please. You'll be
right here until Grandma comes to collect you, won't
you, Eve?'

'Of course she will.' Anthea was clearly puzzled.

So was Kirsty.

'I don't——' Kirsty started.

'I want to see you, Dr Maine,' Reid said harshly. 'I
need to talk to you alone. Now.'

Reid's words had been barely civil while they were
with Anthea and Eve, but as soon as the ward door
closed behind them the façade slipped entirely.

'Do you know what you're about?' he demanded coldly. 'I hope to hell you can afford to pay her.'

Kirsty bit her lip. She was walking down the deserted corridor in front of Reid. Now she stopped, but she didn't turn to face him.

'Of course I can afford to pay her.'

'If you take her for a ride. . .'

Oh, for heaven's sake. Kirsty wheeled around. 'Reid Haslett, what the heck do you think I am?'

'I haven't a clue,' he said roughly. 'But if you're using Anthea Watts to gain my good opinion. . .'

For a moment Kirsty didn't believe she had heard right. She stared. 'I beg your pardon?'

'If you're using Anthea——'

He got no further. The stillness of the little hospital was broken by the sound of a stinging slap.

Kirsty stared in horror at the man in front of her. Her eyes fell to her hand, smarting where it had come into contact with Reid Haslett's face.

'You are a complete toad,' she whispered.

CHAPTER SIX

REID caught up with her before she had gone three steps outside the hospital main doors.

Kirsty was crying. Tears were running helplessly down her face—tears of frustration and anger and—and she didn't know what. No matter what she did, this man prejudged her and found her wanting. And for some crazy, illogical reason it was breaking her heart.

'Kirsty, wait. . .'

Kirsty ignored his urgent plea. Her tears and distress made her clumsy, however. She stumbled on the bottom step and would have fallen. Reid's hands caught her from behind and steadied her.

'Kirsty, listen. . . Kirsty. . .'

Kirsty stiffened. She knew what was coming. An apology. A meaningless apology of words, and then back to insults.

'I have to go,' she managed. She didn't turn. She didn't move. Her body was rigid in his grasp. He was behind her and that was how it was going to stay. 'I haven't had my dinner. I'm tired and I'm hungry and I've had enough. I should say I'm sorry I hit you, but I'm darned if I'm going to say sorry to you ever again, Reid Haslett. You've insulted me in every conceivable way. And why you'd think I'm using someone to buy your good opinion. . . Why you think your opinion of me matters one whit. . .'

It did. For some stupid reason it did.

'Come and we'll find something to eat,' Reid said gently.

'We. . .' Kirsty's voice broke on a sob. 'We! Why would *we* want to do anything together? There's no *we*, Reid Haslett. *Me*. And *you*. And as much distance between us as I can manage.'

He swung her around to face him. Kirsty resisted, but her slender frame was no match for his strength.

If a nurse had looked out of the hospital window then, heaven knew what she would have thought. Two lovers standing under the pale moon? Kirsty let the thought flicker through her distress. She pulled back, but was held.

'Kirsty. . .'

'Let me go.'

'Not until you've heard me out.'

Kirsty looked up at him then. His face was drawn and weary, the skin stretched taut over the finely chiselled bones. His dark eyes were haunted.

'Kirsty, I need to talk to you. I need to have this thing out.'

'What thing?' Kirsty asked breathlessly, but she already knew. The Stephanie thing. Her resurrection as a ghost of someone she didn't know.

'We can't talk here.'

'No.' Kirsty laughed mirthlessly. 'We can't talk anywhere.'

'I've a flat behind the hospital. Come and have dinner with me.'

'You have to be joking.'

'No.' His voice was flat and tired. 'I'm not joking, Kirsty. I'm asking you to help me get this relationship on to some sort of even keel. My grandfather was buried today and every time I turn around, my ex-wife is looking at me. I can't spend the rest of your time in Woongarra treating you as Stephanie. Therefore. . . Therefore I have to get to know you as a colleague.'

Reid ran his hand through his hair. It was a gesture of near-exhaustion.

'Look, you called me a toad,' he said slowly. 'I agree that I've treated you appallingly. I need to sit down and talk to you about medicine for a while. I need to find out about Kirsty Maine, veterinary surgeon. I need to start treating you as a professional associate instead of a woman—and I'm asking you to help me do that.

So stay. I'll cook us both a steak and you can tell me about yourself.' He took a deep breath. 'I'd very much appreciate it, Dr Maine.'

'We tried this once before.'

'I know.' Once more that habitual running of long fingers through ruffled hair. 'And it didn't get me far, did it?' He smiled suddenly, his mouth twisting into a mocking grimace. 'I can't do much worse, though, can I, Kirsty?'

She was a fool. Kirsty stood looking up at him in the dim light. Her car was parked twenty yards away. She should get into her car and drive away as fast as she could. Break a few speed limits, even. If she was really sensible maybe she'd even pack up entirely from Woongarra and never come back. Leave Woongarra with a doctor and not a vet. Because the two were incompatible. . .

Instead she looked into those deep, troubled eyes and her heart wrenched within her.

'I'm tired of being the butt of your anger,' she whispered.

'I know that. It won't happen.'

'A whole meal without an insult?' Kirsty tried to laugh. 'It had better be a short one, then. A sandwich and coffee standing up.'

'I have steak marinating as we speak,' Reid told her firmly. 'There's plenty for two. And you can go home when you like. . .'

Don't do it, her head yelled, and yet something in the way Reid looked at her tore at her so much she couldn't refuse. She couldn't. . .

So Kirsty finally nodded, her head telling her she was a darned fool and her heart telling her she had never been so confused in her life.

Reid's flat was immediately behind the hospital. They had to walk around the veranda to reach it, and Kirsty was achingly aware of the sound of two sets of shoes on the wide, polished veranda-boards.

If the nursing staff were looking. . . The last thing she wanted in this town was to be branded as associated with Reid Haslett. The town was already talking of her similarity to Stephanie. They'd have a field-day with this.

Reid didn't speak. He didn't touch her. They walked side by side, until he stopped to open the screen door and stand aside as she preceded him into his apartment.

Reid's home was strongly masculine. Stephanie had never lived here, Kirsty thought. It was almost deliberately devoid of anything that could be construed as feminine. There were no rugs on the floor. The furniture was old wood or padded leather. Bookcases lined the walls and Kirty's eyes flicked over the titles with nervous attention. Medical texts. Travel. Science fiction. Poetry. . .

Poetry. Her gaze swung back to Reid. There was so much about this man that she didn't know. The romance poets were well-represented. Byron. Shelley. Robert Burns, for heaven's sake. She lifted a slim volume from where it lay on the arm of a leather armchair.

'You're reading this at the moment?' she asked.

Reid had walked across to the refrigerator. Now he paused and looked across at the book she was holding.

'Re-reading,' he said shortly.

'He's a favourite of mine,' Kirsty told him. Robbie Burns was a poet she had read again and again, finding comfort in the lilt of the words as much as their content.

'Really?' Reid's eyebrows lifted, and Kirsty could tell he didn't believe her.

'"O wad some Pow'r the giftie gie us To see oursels as others see us!"' Kirsty quoted the words softly, her eyes on Reid. 'I don't know how you see me, Reid Haslett. It seems you hate me, but I don't know why.'

'I don't hate you.' He was staring at her. 'You really do read poetry!'

'Should I not?' Kirsty laid down the book. 'You don't see me reading poetry?'

'Not many vets. . .'

Kirsty shook her head. 'Not many Stephanies.'

He stared for a moment longer, and the expression in his eyes told Kirsty she was right. The wounds Stephanie had inflicted on this man were still raw and new, and her likeness to his ex-wife was something he couldn't escape from.

'How's your mother?' she asked gently.

Reid turned to the stove. He lit the gas, greased the pan, and then carefully lowered the steak on to the sizzling iron. It took about two minutes before he answered her question.

'Asleep, I hope,' he said shortly. 'I gave her a sedative for the night.' Then he gave a rueful smile. 'She's almost ashamed of being upset—my grandfather's been ill for so long. But they've been very close. She seems to think it's an admission of defeat to take any medication—so I told her she was only to take a sedative the night she buried her father. Would you like a drink?'

'No, thank you.' One glass of wine and she'd go to sleep where she stood, Kirsty thought. Or cry. That was the way she was feeling.

'There's everything we need for a salad in the fridge. How about you put one together while I tend the steak?'

'I can do that.' They were circling each other like wary dogs.

She crossed to the bench. It was almost a relief to do something.

'You don't live with your mother, then?'

'Not since I was eighteen.' He smiled. 'And that was a way back, quoth the grey-beard. About sixteen years back.'

'So your arrival the night your grandfather died was just fortuitous?'

'No. My grandfather had advanced heart failure. I'd

been out there night and morning for weeks. We were expecting. . . We were expecting what happened.'

'Do you do many house-calls?'

'Not as many as you'll do.' Reid flashed a searching look at her. 'If you're any good the farmers will start using you twenty-four hours a day.'

'And they don't use you?'

'Oh, I'm in use.' Reid flipped the steak expertly. 'But when Dr Maine's patients feel ill they tend to lie down in the paddock, roll their eyes and moan. Mine are more inclined to telephone the ambulance and come into my nice, comfortable hospital—especially when a house-call fifteen miles out means that the hospital's without a doctor for that time if I go. This place really needs two doctors—but it doesn't stand a chance of getting them.'

'Because Woongarra's so isolated?'

'Because Woongarra's so isolated,' Reid agreed. 'So why didn't the isolation deter Kirsty Maine?'

Kirsty concentrated on shredding her lettuce.

'I wanted to come here.'

'Why?'

Kirsty shrugged. 'A dream, I suppose. To become a country vet.'

'A dream. . .' Still those eyes were boring into her. 'You're a bit old for dreaming, aren't you, Dr Maine?'

'Am I?'

Reid didn't answer. He collected two plates and flipped the steak on to them. 'Salad ready?'

Kirsty looked doubtfully down at her lettuce and tomato offering. 'Such as it is.'

'Reid smiled. 'Never mind. The steak will make up for it.'

It did. It was superb—or maybe that was just because Kirsty was hungry.

'Were you going to eat all of this?' she asked dubiously. There was enough steak on her plate to feed one and a half of her, and the steak on Reid's plate was bigger.

'My housekeeper thinks I'm fading to a shadow,' Reid grinned. 'Besides, the hospital pays for my food, and anything I don't eat the housekeeper gets to take home. Hence I get fed excessively.'

'Sounds corrupt to me.'

'The incorruptible Dr Maine. . .' Then at Kirsty's look, Reid held up a hand. 'OK. I'm sorry. My sarcastic tongue has to stay inside my sarcastic head.'

'It'd be nice,' Kirsty said drily.

'You don't think I can keep it up?'

'It'd surprise me.'

He looked at her again then, his eyes following the etched lines of strain around her eyes. 'You're tired.'

'I guess I can't be as tired as you.' Kirsty pushed her plate back. 'But you're right. I need my bed. Soon I'll have a receptionist and things will be better.'

'I guess they will.' Reid had risen also. 'Would you like coffee?'

Kirsty shook her head. The atmosphere was changing and she wasn't sure. . . She knew she had to go, and fast. He was too darned close. Too darned big.

'I can drive myself out to your mother's on Saturday,' she told him. 'There's no need for you to collect me.'

'It's a waste taking two cars.'

'But you're not coming.'

'Yes, I am.'

Kirsty's eyes flicked up to his in surprise. 'But you said——'

'I think I've changed my mind,' Reid said softly. 'A man has the right to change his mind—especially when he thinks he might be making a bloody huge mistake.'

Reid didn't elaborate. He just walked back out to her car. They hadn't reached the vehicle, however, before the main doors of the hospital were flung wide and a nurse came out.

'Dr Haslett?' She was peering into the dim light at the edge of the car-park. 'Is that you?'

'I'm here, Eileen.'

'There's been a call. A fire. . .'

Kirsty's hand was on the doorhandle of her car. Now she paused.

'Someone's hurt?' Reid demanded.

'They don't know yet. But it's the Henderson farm. It's started in the stables and the fire chief says it's big. He asks if you can go out.'

'Tell him I'm on my way. Who's on ambulance duty?'

'Sam. I'll ring him now.'

'Tell him I'll meet him there.' Reid's voice was commanding and sure—the voice of a man accustomed to taking charge. He looked down at Kirsty. 'The Hendersons own a horse-stud out past Anthea's. If the stables are on fire, the horses. . .'

'Of course I'll come,' Kirsty agreed, knowing what he was asking before the request was voiced.

'Come in my car. It'll be faster.'

'No.' Kirsty shook her head. 'All my gear's in the back of mine. If there are injured horses. . .'

'What I want will be in the ambulance.' Reid was thinking fast. 'I'll drive your car, then, Dr Maine. It's back-roads and I know the way. Let's go.'

Kirsty's little car had never been driven so fast. She clung to the seat like a reluctant car-rally passenger. The gravel roads accentuated the speed, but Reid's driving was skilled and sure. He wasn't taking unnecessary risks, but he was getting there fast.

'It's a wonder Bob Henderson hasn't checked you out already,' Reid told her as they sped through the night. 'He was tickled pink there's a new vet coming. His property is an excellent stud facility and it's costing him a fortune to use the Bega vets. He's expanding too. Last time I was there he was building new sheds.' Reid frowned. 'How on earth. . .?'

They saw the fire well before they reached it. The night was a mass of brilliant orange, shooting skyward. As they topped a rise allowing them to see into the valley below, Kirsty drew in her breath in horror.

The farm was huge. By the light of the brilliant flames she could see a vast farmhouse and acres of shedding. All the shedding to the north of the house seemed to be burning.

'There's normally up to thirty thoroughbred mares in those stables at one time,' Reid said grimly. 'Bob's had trouble with theft and interference with the horses so he brings the champion bloodstock in at night. The ones he really values, that is. The place is full of mares about to foal. And High Born's here at stud.'

'High Born. . .' Kirsty gasped. '*The* High Born?'

Most of the world had heard of High Born. The stallion had made a fortune for his owners on the turf, completing three brilliant seasons before being put to stud. She looked down again at the flames. 'Well, I hope to heaven he's not in those north stables,' Kirsty whispered. 'Oh, dear God. . .'

The scene was something out of a nightmare. Reid drove the car to the main gate and stopped. The ambulance was bearing down behind them, siren screaming. Reid flagged it to a halt. 'We'll leave the car unlocked,' he told Kirsty briefly. 'Send someone back for your gear if you need it. The less vehicles in the yard the better.'

Two minutes later they were in the yard, surrounded by fire, noise and confusion.

Reid was grabbed fast by the fire chief. The man knew exactly who Reid was and he needed him.

'You're wanted over here, Doc,' the fire chief yelled. 'Bob Henderson's here.' The sound of the fire was all-enveloping, creating its own wind. 'He collapsed trying to get the mares out.'

A man was lying on the grass in the midst of the yard. Reid crossed swiftly, ignoring the chaos around him. Kirsty followed, unsure where to start.

Bob Henderson was lying crouched over, and even above the noise of the fire Kirsty could hear the awful tones of someone having life-threatening trouble breathing. Each breath was a rasping, fought-for wheeze. In the ghastly firelight the man's face was white as death under his soot- and smoke-stained skin, and as Reid knelt and helped him move on to his side the eyes staring up at him were rolling in terror.

'OK, Bob. You'll be right now.' Reid's hand was on the man's wrist, the other ripping open the buttons of his shirt. 'Trying to fight fires when your asthma's not controlled at the best of times is a fool's job. We'll just get some oxygen back into your lungs and you'll feel a hundred percent.'

The man's terror didn't abate. He clutched feebly at Reid and fought for another breath.

Reid looked around for Sam, the ambulance driver, but he had disappeared from view. Kirsty was next in line.

'Get me oxygen, Kirsty,' Reid snapped. 'Fast. It's in the ambulance. There's a nasal tube. You'll find it in the left-hand locker. I need cortisone... aminophylline... Where the hell's Sam?'

Kirsty was already running. The ambulance was wide open and lit from within. Where *was* the ambulance driver? She looked around fleetingly as she ran and saw his uniform, crouched over someone else to the side of the ambulance. There was more than one casualty, then...

The oxygen first... Kirsty located what Reid needed swiftly. There was a small black doctor's bag on the floor of the van. A doctor's bag... It had to contain syringes and pumps and the drugs Reid needed. An acute asthma attack was something every doctor's bag would be equipped to deal with. She gathered her collection to her and ran through the mass of hoses and shouting men to where Reid's patient lay.

He was getting worse. Bob Henderson had slumped back, and his colour was dreadful. Kirsty had been fitting the intra-nasal tube to the oxygen as she ran, and she shoved it into Reid's hand. Two seconds later it was inserted into Bob's nostrils and the oxygen was released.

'Aminophylline. . .' Reid was half talking to himself.

'Is it in your bag?' Kirsty looked desperately into the depths of the leather case. She couldn't see. . .

A few feet away a woman was standing, staring uselessly at the fire, and in her hand she held a torch. Kirsty moved fast. The woman turned and made a slight murmur of protest but Kirsty had already grabbed the torch and swung it back down towards Reid's bag.

Reid hadn't waited. He was groping in the dim light and now, in the torch's beam, he located what he had been searching for. Cortisone and aminophylline were both swiftly syringed intravenously into Bob's hastily swabbed arm.

'I'm putting up a drip,' Reid muttered. He looked around again. 'Where the hell is Sam? I want Bob in the ambulance, and out of this damned smoke.'

'I can——'

'Get me Sam!'

Fine. Kirsty stood, acknowledging that Sam would be a swifter, surer stretcher-bearer than she. 'I know where he is,' she told Reid. 'I'll get him.' Reid was already turning back to his patient.

'Just relax now, Bob. The oxygen's working and we've injected what we need to get things under control. The only danger now is panic. Try and breathe slowly. Relax. . .'

'Relax. . .' Bob moaned. 'How the hell can I. . .?'

But Kirsty was gone.

There were two sets of stables, the main one of which was well alight. The whole north line of stables was burning fiercely. Across the mounting-yard was the second set of stables, as yet untouched by fire. They faced back towards the burning stables, however, and Kirsty sent up a silent prayer that the horses from those had also been taken to safety. Any horse facing that sight would be mad with terror.

Sam was where Kirsty had just seen him. He was kneeling beside an elderly man. The man was crouched over, his head in his arms.

'Sam?' Sam looked up. 'Dr Haslett needs you,' Kirsty told him. 'He needs the stretcher and a drip-holder.' She looked uncertainly down at the man Sam had been tending. 'Can I help here?'

Sam stood and shook his head. 'Doc Haslett'll have to see him, but it can wait. Where is he?'

Kirsty motioned to Reid's location and Sam disappeared into the chaos. Kirsty looked doubtfully down at his deserted patient.

'Is there something. . .?'

The man looked up then, his grimed face lit by the dreadful orange glow of the fire.

'I've broke my arm,' he muttered. 'Sam says it's busted, good and proper.'

Kirsty sank to her knees beside him. 'The doctor's here,' she told him. 'We'll get you some pain relief. . .'

He pulled away from her. 'Leave it, girl,' he said roughly. 'It'll wait.'

Kirsty looked at the man's haggard face. Was this man a part-owner? Something was wrong besides a broken arm. 'How were you hurt?' she tried.

'High Born. . .' The man's voice broke on a sob. 'They won't. . .they can't get him out. I tried, but he won't let me near him. Bob's the only one—and Bob can't——'

Kirsty stared back at the stables. 'You mean there's a horse still in there?'

'In the south stable. The one that's not burnt yet. They've decided he'll have to stay. There's no way he'll come out. But. . .I've tried. The bloody horse reared up and broke my bloody arm. He's insured, but. . . Oh, God, it'd break your bloody heart.'

Kirsty was staring at the south stables. They weren't burning. . .yet! Sparks were showering down on to the roof. The firemen were directing their hoses at the building, trying to damp it down, but it was so close. . .

There was a line of shedding running along the side
of the mounting-yard, forming the base of a 'U' with
both lines of stables. It had caught at one end.

And there was still a horse inside. High Born. . .

'The smoke's too bad to get close? Is that how Bob
Henderson lost consciousness?'

The man stared at her as though dazed. Finally the
question penetrated. 'No,' he managed. 'The smoke's
not that bad in there yet. The wind seems to be pulling
it in the other direction. Bob was getting the last horses
out of the shed that's burning now. He was affected
before we tried to get High Born. We left the south
stable till last because we thought we had time. By
then, though—well, there was so much noise and
smoke High Born was terrified. He's the only one in
the south stable—on account of getting too damned
excited when the mares, or the geldings either for that
matter, are anywhere near him. But he's mad
with fear.'

'Are you fit to show me?' Kirsty demanded.

The man's eyes stared up at her.

'I'm a vet,' Kirsty said firmly. 'I've dealt with frightened horses before. Maybe I'll——'

'You haven't got a hope.'

'At least let me try.'

He looked up at her, and the despair in his eyes
didn't lessen.

'I'll show you.'

High Born was at the far end of a long line of stabling.
The man—whose name was Fred—led the way behind
the building to where a gap in the 'U' led them through
to High Born's box. Fred was still cradling his arm,
and his face under the grime was ghastly.

The smoke was awful. At the other side of the
U-shape of buildings, flames were rising in a sheet.
Men were working frantically to get water on the
wall—shouting to each other through the smoke.
Water sprayed back over Kirsty as they entered the

gap, and Kirsty realised they hadn't given up on the building yet.

'They're trying to save it with High Born inside,' Fred gasped between coughing. 'It's his only hope. But he'll choke on the smoke, I reckon—or die of shock.'

'Or kill himself by throwing himself about,' Kirsty agreed. She had a handkerchief to her mouth but it wasn't making breathing much easier.

The stallion was still confined in his box. Kirsty heard him before she saw him. His screams filled the night, and his flailing hooves hit the wooden sides of his box over and over.

Kirsty peered through the smoke, trying desperately to get her bearings. The nearest flames were a hundred yards away. Safe enough to get High Born out, if only they could calm the horse.

'He won't come,' Fred said desperately. 'He can see the flames.'

'We can't break through the rear of his box?' If they could move the horse backwards, away from the flames, he'd go much more willingly.

'We've been planning new stabling at the rear of this line. There's a line of solid reinforcement—fire-bricks. We'd never smash through without the horse thrashing himself to bits in fear.'

Kirsty's mind was racing. They weren't going to get High Born out while he could see what he was facing. Smoke, fire, terror. . .

He didn't have to go far, though. He was at the end of the line of stables—right next to the gap.

If they could block the view. . .

Maybe. . .

Three boxes along, one box had been left free of horses and filled with dry feed. It was packed with bales of lucerne hay. If she could shift some. . .

'It'd burn. . .' She was talking out loud.

'What?' Fred sounded as confused as Kirsty was feeling. But a plan was forming. . .

The hay-bales. . .

'Go and talk to him,' she told Fred. 'Don't go into his box. Don't try to touch him. Just stand in front of him, block as much of his view as you can and talk him down. There's time. Keep the panic right out of your voice.'

Fred stared through the smoke. 'But——'

'I'm going to block his view completely,' Kirsty said. 'It's the only way.'

She had to form an L-shaped wall, eighteen hands high. She had to form a passage for High Born to walk through and out. A makeshift passage of hay bales. . .

There was a hose attached to the tap beside High Born's box. Water pressure? Kirsty turned the tap without much hope, but a strong stream of water spurted out.

'It's attached to a tank at the back,' Fred said grimly, seeing her surprise. 'We've mains water as well, and the firemen have their own supply. . .'

'Thank you. . .' Kirsty sent a scanty prayer upward and shoved the hose into Fred's hands. 'Hold this. Don't move with it or you'll startle the horse, but as I put each bale on my pile you make damned sure it's too wet to catch fire. Otherwise we'll be building a funeral pyre. . .'

Bales of hay were heavy at the best of times. As a student Kirsty had spent a summer baling hay. Her arms remembered, and groaned with the memory of their weight.

The first few bales were reasonably easy. Kirsty hauled the bundles of lucerne and dragged them into the passage. It took ten bales to form the base of the L-shaped corridor, and the bales were maybe eighteen inches high. Kirsty glanced back at the stallion. He was a good eighteen hands. She'd have to make the wall two bales thick or it wouldn't be stable higher up. How many bales did that make?

The stallion had ceased his frantic rearing. Fred stood leaning against the wall, giving some relief, Kirsty guessed, to his injured shoulder. His good hand directed the hose. His shaky voice continued as Kirsty worked, deliberately raised to superimpose himself on the noise of the fire.

'Good fella. There's nothing to be afraid of. We'll get you out of here, no sweat. You see this lady? She's the new vet. A woman vet, for God's sake. Don't say I hold with 'em, but she looks pretty enough, and she's doing the right thing by us, old mate. Now you just settle down and take it easy. Watch a woman at work. And when she's finished we'll take you out in the paddock, away from all this damned smoke.'

Kirsty couldn't suppress a grin. 'Watch a woman at work. . .'

A couple of firemen had seen what she was doing. They had emerged from nowhere and were now periodically spraying her wall from the other side as they soaked the unburnt building. She blessed them. The heat from the fire was enough to make the bales burst into spontaneous combustion.

She heaved another bale higher. Five bales high. . .

'Kirsty!'

Kirsty swung to the gap at the end of her makeshift corridor. Reid was holding a torch in his hand, fighting to see in the gloom. 'What the hell do you think you're doing?'

'I'm getting a horse out,' she snapped. 'I have to get enough hay up to block his view of the flames. Put that damned thing out and keep your voice down.'

Reid's torch flicked around and found Fred. The arc of light caught High Born, and he whinnied and reared back.

'Easy now,' Fred said nervously. 'Don't let the good doctor upset you. Look, he hasn't a needle or suppository in sight.'

Kirsty choked with laughter, but her laughter turned into an exhausted cough. Her wall was growing too high for her to heave the hay up. If only she could throw the bales. . .

'You get on top,' Reid said swiftly. He had taken

in the whole scene at a glance and was striding into the box where the hay was stored.

'On top. . .' Kirsty stared at him.

'On top of your damned wall. I'll throw the bales up. We'll have it done in minutes.'

'But Bob. . .'

'He's OK for the moment. Sam's with him and knows where I am. Let's keep working, Dr Maine. If you've started this then you might as well finish it.'

Three minutes later the wall was complete. The last bale dropped into place and the flames from the other section of the stables disappeared as if by magic. Not the smoke, though. It was getting thicker by the minute.

'OK.' Kirsty clambered down from her eyrie. She jumped the last few feet and Reid's hands came out to steady her.

It was amazing just how steadying they were. This next bit was hard, and she wasn't sure. . .

'OK, I want you both to go outside the gap,' she said firmly—more firmly than she felt. 'Both of you.'

'But he knows me,' Fred quavered.

'Yes, and he's hurt you already.' Kirsty glanced up at the stallion, still nervously pacing in its box. With the overhead lighting off, Kirsty would normally be in darkness here. Reid had his torch turned firmly off. The flame from the burning buildings was so intense, though, that it was indirectly lighting the whole scene. She could feel heat burning into her body. There was no time to wait. 'You won't be able to move fast enough if he kicks. Now go.'

'Kirsty, don't be a damned fool.' It was Reid, his voice astounded. 'You can't——'

'Don't tell me my job, Dr Haslett,' Kirsty snapped. 'Thank you for your help. Fred has a broken arm. I suggest he needs the help of a doctor. Leave the horse to the vet.'

'If you think I'll leave you in here. . .'

'You must.' Kirsty cast another nervous glance at

High Born. 'You don't have a choice, Dr Haslett. One person taking it quietly is his only chance.'

A crash outside shattered the stillness. High Born snorted and his head tossed, but he didn't rear. Fred had done his work well.

'Good lad,' Kirsty said softly, walking slowly, slowly towards him. She didn't look at the two men. 'Please. Will you both go?'

And then she ignored them.

'Quiet, boy. Quiet.'

It took all the nerve and patience she possessed not to rush it. Behind her the two men stood indecisive for a long moment. Then Reid lifted his hand and touched her, oh, so lightly, on the shoulder. It was a gesture of blessing, infinitely comforting.

Then he and Fred silently left.

She was alone.

'I'd be scared, too, if I were you,' Kirsty said conversationally, addressing herself totally to the terrified stallion. 'I'm not much into fires. I'm not much into anything requiring bravery, if the truth be known. You should see me when I have to go to the dentist.'

The big horse was looking straight at her, its ears flattened back and its nostrils flared. She had a way to go.

'Of course, I haven't been to the dentist now for years. That's how silly I am. I bet you'd be braver than me. I'll just bet you would, you great big beautiful boy. Come on now, darling. Trust me. You can trust me.'

Slowly, slowly Kirsty opened the lower door of the stables. Her eyes held the big horse all the time.

She desperately wanted to cough. Her eyes were streaming and her throat was raw. Instead she forced herself to put away the handkerchief over her mouth. She had to be normal. Normal in a nightmare. . .

Another crash from outside. Kirsty didn't budge— her voice didn't change from the same calm, soothing tone.

'Come on, big boy. You don't want to stay in this rotten place. The paddock's green and lush, and the air there's damp, with no rotten smoke in it. I bet you could do with a lovely drink of water too. Come on, darling boy. Come on.'

Her hand lifted, ever so slowly, and found his halter. His ears flattened again, he clattered back. . .

'It's OK, my big boy.' Kirsty moved back with him. If he reared now. . .

Kirsty was in no doubt as to what would happen if he reared. This was a big horse. He could hurl her around the stable if he wanted.

'It's OK. . .'

And his hooves stayed magically on the ground. High Born stood, his whole body trembling under her hand, but his eyes were trusting.

'Let's get out of here,' Kirsty said softly. She ran a hand lightly over his muzzle in a gesture meant to reassure him that there was all the time in the world. 'Come on, my lovely boy. . .' And she led him out of his box, along the makeshift corridor, and then out through the gap and into the night.

Her last fear was the yard. When Kirsty had last gone through the gap, the yard had been all frantic, noisy chaos. How would High Born react? He'd bolt, she thought. But at least it was better than letting him die in the stables.

Instead, Fred and Reid had prepared the way. They must have watched for her coming. The moment she emerged, the yard fell silent, apart from the roar of the flames. The way was clear across to the paddock, and Fred was signalling her, showing her the way to go. Kirsty led the stallion across, her feet breaking into a light run as she felt the stallion's nervous energy build. Now was not the time for a lesson in good manners.

A moment later he was through the first gate, then the second. At a signal from Fred, Kirsty loosened her hold of his halter, and he cantered away into the night.

This was the house paddock. It was up-wind from the fire. Here he was safe.

'He really should be rubbed down,' she said worriedly as she turned back to Fred. 'He's been sweating.'

'It's a warm night,' Fred reassured her. 'He'll do no harm.' He hesitated. 'Well done, lass. There's not a lot of men could do what you just did and that's the truth.'

'All the other horses are safe?' Kirsty asked.

'They are.' The man hesitated. 'Though. . . There's a mare over at the house gate we'd be grateful if you could look at. There's a couple of lads with her now. She smashed her hock into the wall when the fire first broke out, and it's gashed deep, like.'

'I'll do that.' Kirsty hesitated, looking around, and Reid materialised from nowhere. He'd stayed out of the stallion's sight as Kirsty had led him across the yard—an easy thing to do. It was hard to see more than four feet in the smoke and darkness.

'You can leave the horses to Dr Maine now, Fred,' Reid said severely. 'She's shown you she's more than capable of looking after them. Now, let's see that arm.'

'But. . .'

'Dr Haslett's right,' Kirsty told him. 'Leave them to me. I'll take care of them.'

A stable-hand appeared, leading the injured mare. Kirsty inspected the gash by torchlight and decided reluctantly that repair couldn't wait. Luckily the gash was a lateral incision across the hock. If it had been otherwise. . . Well, no use making her life harder by imagining difficulties. She had enough as it was.

This horse, too, was nervous. Kirsty finally elected to take her down well past the house, and behind a stand of gums in a far paddock. It was a long way to lead an injured mare, but it meant she could calm the horse before she stitched. She didn't want to have to sedate her at her late stage of pregnancy—not on top of everything else the mare had been through.

The two lads helping her seemed almost as

frightened as the horse. One offered to hold the lantern as she worked, but Kirsty finally chose to place it on the ground, the boy's hands shook so much.

The dim light actually helped. The small area where Kirsty worked was illuminated but the mare seemed hardly aware of what Kirsty was doing to her leg. There was too much else to worry about. The two lads held and soothed her, but the mare was worried about the fire. The smoke filled her nostrils. It was the fire that was the peril—not the vet working swiftly beside her hindquarters.

By the time Kirsty finished stitching and helped rub the frightened mare down, she was exhausted. Her dressing was makeshift to say the least.

'I'll come back and put a spica dressing on her tomorrow,' she told the boys. 'Is there any safe stabling you can use tonight?'

'There's one stable next to the house. . . As far as we can tell it's in no danger.'

'Walk her gently until you're sure it's safe,' Kirsty told them. 'Then put her there for the night.'

The fire had died down to a faint, fiery heap. As Kirsty walked back around the house she was appalled at what she saw.

The stables were gone. High Born had been moved just in time. The whole U-shape of buildings around the mounting-yard were a glowing heap of ashes—including Kirsty's makeshift corridor.

A woman approached, bearing a steaming mug of tea. Kirsty took it gratefully and stood in the midst of the yard, slowly drinking as she watched the firemen methodically mopping up the last of the embers.

'It'd break your heart, wouldn't it,' the woman said. She peered closer at Kirsty. 'You must be the new vet.'

'Yes.'

'I have a message for you.' The woman held out a hand. 'I'm Doreen, a neighbour of the Hendersons. Dr Haslett says he's taken Fred and Bob into the hospital with the ambulance, so he doesn't need a ride home.'

'I assumed that.' Kirsty hesitated. 'Have you heard how Mr Henderson is?'

'Dr Haslett's keeping him for the night, of course,' the woman told her. 'I gather his asthma improved once he got out of the smoke. Irene—Mrs Henderson—is in there, too. Suffering from shock, she was. Dr Haslett's put her to bed in hospital, too.'

Bed. . . It was starting to sound like a dream—more tempting than any exotic holiday. Bed. . .

Kirsty handed back the mug. 'Tell them. . . Tell whoever's in charge here that I'll come out first thing in the morning and run a check over all the horses,' she said unsteadily. 'For now. . . For now I'm going home.'

Bed. . . Kirsty headed towards her pillows like an automaton. She'd showered and was walking from the bathroom to the bed when something hit her window. Kirsty hesitated and then shrugged. Whatever it was, she was too tired to care. Bed. . .

The sound came again. It sounded like small stones being thrown against the glass. And again. . .

For heaven's sake. . . It was three in the morning. She didn't need anything else. . .

Kirsty crossed to the window and pulled it wide. Below the house, in the light of the garden lamp Anthea left on all night as security, stood Reid.

Reid. . .

Kirsty instinctively pulled the flimsy fabric of her nightgown closer. What on earth. . .?

She couldn't call out. To wake Eve and her grandmother at this hour should result in her being thrown out on her ear. And then, before she had a chance to do anything, Reid had moved swiftly out of the lamplight. There was a small scraping noise underneath, a hand appeared on the balcony rail, and then Reid's head appeared.

'Hell,' he said conversationally. 'It's not as easy as it looks, is it?'

Kirsty's lower lip trembled. She wasn't sure whether to scream for help or to giggle.

'Some ladies. . .' Once more that conversational tone. Reid was having trouble hauling himself over the rail. 'Some ladies seeing a man about to fall to his doom would lend a hand.'

'Some ladies might,' Kirsty said cautiously. 'But some ladies might want to know what's in it for them.'

'Mercenary wretch.' With a final heave the rest of Reid's body appeared. He pulled himself over the balcony and sank to a sitting position on the wooden balcony floor. He looked up at Kirsty accusingly. 'Did you have to have a second-floor window?'

'I arranged it to keep intruders out.' Keep it light, she told herself. It was hard; her voice wasn't quite working. 'Look, Reid, if you think you're playing Romeo to my Juliet. . .'

'I don't think anything of the kind.' With an effort Reid hauled himself to his feet. 'Have you any idea just how tired I am?'

'Nearly as tired as I am, I reckon.' Kirsty's hands were pulling together the low neckline of her nightdress. Why don't I wear flannel? she was asking herself.

'You can't possibly be as tired as me.' He crossed to her then, and his hands took hers, pulling them away from her protective stance. 'Don't worry, Kirsty, love. I'm not here for rape and pillage.'

'What. . .? What are you here for?'

He stood, looking down at her in the moonlight, and his eyes reflected the questioning in hers. Maybe he didn't know.

'What you did tonight. . .' His eyes held hers, as if he couldn't break away. 'I had to tell you. What you did was the bravest——'

'No!'

'The bravest,' he went on inexorably. 'Fred told Bob

Henderson what you'd done and Bob broke down and wept. That stallion's the pride of his heart. And Kirsty. . .'

'Y-yes.'

Kirsty's breathing was coming too fast.

'I couldn't go to bed without telling you. I think you're a hell of a woman, Kirsty Maine.'

'You're kidding.' She stared blankly up at him. 'You don't even like me, Reid Haslett.'

'Liking has nothing to do with it.' And he bent and kissed her.

Kirsty had no energy left to protest. She had no energy—and no desire. . . No desire to protest, that was.

It must be fatigue, she thought fleetingly. It must be fatigue that was stopping her fighting away from him. This was a kiss of weariness—a kiss of battles overcome—of shared effort and of triumph.

His lips moved strongly on hers and the fatigue lessened. The desire stayed.

It was a kiss of healing. And it was a kiss that held the promise of love.

The kiss lingered on. Neither wanted it to end. Reid's hands held her to him, his strength warming her, caressing her. Below the balcony, a tree-frog muttered grunts of encouragement, and Kirsty Maine's heart stirred within.

And then he was putting her from him, his arms holding her at full length.

'Dear God,' he said unsteadily. 'Kirsty. . .'

She stared up at him, her eyes wide and troubled. With the distance between them came remembrance.

Neil. . . What was she doing? Oh, Neil, she mustn't forget. . .

'I think you'd better go,' Kirsty whispered.

There was remembrance in his eyes, too. 'I think. . .I think you're right.'

They stared at each other for a long, long moment in the pale moonlight.

It had to end. It had to. What her body was telling her had to be ignored.

'Good. . . Goodnight, Reid,' she whispered falteringly. Then, as if making a supreme effort, Kirsty turned away from the man before her. Without another glance she walked back into her bedroom and closed the balcony door behind her.

Juliet would never have done such a thing. But then, her time as Juliet was long past.

CHAPTER SEVEN

KIRSTY slept fitfully for three hours. At dawn it was almost a relief to realise her day could start. She no longer had to lie on her soft pillows with her heart aching for something she had sworn she would never want again.

She ate toast and coffee in the deserted kitchen, left a note for Eve and her grandmother, and then drove slowly out to the Henderson farm.

The place looked dismal in the daylight.

The yard was a sea of mud and ash. A fire engine was still there, with a couple of firemen desultorily drinking tea and watching the smouldering ruins. Apart from that, there was no one.

'Don't you believe in sleep, Doc?' one of the firemen asked her, recognising her from the night before.

'How about you?' Kirsty countered, and the fireman grinned.

'I get relieved in a couple of hours and I go home to bed.'

'Half your luck.' She wasn't really jealous, though, Kirsty reflected. The last thing she wanted at the moment was to be idle. The last thing she wanted was time to think.

'The stable-hands have just turned in to get some sleep themselves,' the fireman told her. 'They rubbed down all the horses before hitting the sack—just to make sure none of them was carrying an injury they ought to know about. They asked if you'd recheck the mare you worked on last night. She's up in the little stable by the house. If you want them, just bang on the house door, but I reckon you'll have to bang hard.'

'I won't do that.'

The only untouched stable was attached to the house—a small shed that had obviously been built to

house a child's favourite pony. Here was the pregnant
mare Kirsty had stitched last night, and Kirsty was
relieved to see her moving well. She took her out of the
stable and ran her for a few yards up and down the yard,
but the mare didn't hesitate to put weight on the injured
leg. No tendon damage, then. . . It had been hard to
stitch such a wound in the dim light and smoke-filled
air—hard to assess the damage accurately.

Kirsty put the mare back in her stable and bathed
and redressed the wound. Normally she'd ask one of
the lads to assist but the mare was quiet, as though
the exertions of the night had been too much. She *was*
very heavily in foal, too. Kirsty applied a proper spica
bandage to allow maximum movement without the
dressing shifting, patted the mare's broad rump and
left her to peace. That was what the pregnant mare
needed more than anything.

Kirsty then walked slowly down to the paddocks
behind the house. Here were all the horses taken from
the stables last night. The men had done a fine job.
The traces of ash and smoke had been brushed from
their coats and they were grazing placidly in the
morning light.

She walked from horse to horse, watching the movement of each as they moved nervously away from her
unaccustomed presence. Some she took the time to
approach, tempting them with soothing words and
pieces of carrot she'd borrowed from Anthea's kitchen.
She ran her eyes expertly over their gleaming coats
and their legs, looking for damage. The men had
checked them but they had been tired, checking in the
dark. It took time to assess each horse carefully, but
the time taken now would be worth it. If any injury—
even a muscle strain—was left. . .

Bob Henderson had been lucky, Kirsty thought an
hour later. There seemed little damage at all.

She turned back to the house and saw High Born,
standing next to the gate in the next paddock.

'Well, well,' she said conversationally. 'Good morning, sir.' Her hand went into a pocket and came out experimentally with a piece of carrot. 'Can I interest you in an after-breakfast snack?'

It seemed she could.

She approached. High Born snorted and flung his head, but he didn't move away.

'I trust none of these ladies are in an interesting condition.' Kirsty smiled. 'And, if they are, I expect you to behave yourself, sir.' The paddock fences were solid but this stallion was strong and determined. It wasn't ideal to have them housed next door to each other.

Who, me? his eyes seemed to say, and Kirsty chuckled.

'Oh, you gorgeous thing.' She ran her hand lightly down his muzzle. 'What I'd give to ride you.'

'You can if you like.'

Kirsty wheeled around. The voice was oh, so familiar—and so close. Reid Haslett was leaning on the gate watching her. In the early morning light, the sun still a pale promise on the horizon, the man leaning nonchalantly on the yard-gate, wearing thigh-hugging jeans, riding-boots and a short-sleeved shirt open almost to the waist, looked impossibly handsome. Too darned handsome for his own good, Kirsty thought angrily, turning back to the stallion.

'Bob Henderson says you can have half his kingdom, and I reckon if you asked it of him this morning he'd give it gladly.' Reid didn't seem to have noticed her discomfort. 'When Bob left here last night he thought High Born was doomed. Saving him has cast the loss of insured stables into the realm of nuisance. I reckon he'll think the odd ride on High Born a small price to pay.'

'I won't ask it of him.' Kirsty smiled reluctantly. She gave High Born another piece of carrot. 'I haven't ridden since——'

'Since when?'

Kirsty's face closed.

'Since I was younger.'

He stood watching her. The morning sun sparkled on the dew-wet grass. The wind might spring up later, but for now it was a perfect morning. The drama of the night was gone. High Born nuzzled Kirsty's face and the world was still.

'Is. . .? Is there any reason you're here?' Kirsty finally managed, breaking the stillness. 'Was anyone else injured?'

'I thought you'd be here,' Reid said softly. 'I came to find you.'

Kirsty's eyes flashed up to his. Colour flooded into her cheeks. She felt about sixteen.

'Wh-why. . .?'

'How are the horses?' he asked non-committally. His voice was warm as the rising sun. His eyes were still on her, and his look was making her colour mount further.

'They're fine.' Kirsty gave High Born a farewell pat of his flank and then turned to walk up to the house. Reid walked with her, as though he had always intended to. 'We were lucky last night was so warm. If it had been cold we would have had more trouble— with the shock and then putting them out in the weather.' She hesitated. 'How. . .? Do they know how the fire started?'

'An electrical fault, they reckon, though it's too soon to be sure. Bob was building new stables behind the ones High Born was in and extended the existing electricity supply. The fire started in the switch-box in the north wing.' Reid reached suddenly and caught Kirsty's arm, causing her to stop. He swung her round to face him. 'Kirsty. . .'

'Yes?' Her face was tight and as non-committal as she could make it.

He stood looking down at her for a long moment, as though trying to make up his mind what he wanted to say. Finally he shook his head.

'Bob Henderson wants to see you,' he said at last.

'He's fretting about his horses. His asthma's still not completely controlled. His blood pressure's too high for comfort and he had a minor infarct two years ago. I don't want him worrying if we can avoid it. He wants to get home this morning, but I want him to stay longer, so I said I'd ask you to drop in on him this morning before you start at your surgery. Your reassurance might help him decide to stay where he is.'

'So that was why you came. . .'

Once more that look.

'Yes,' he said, and his voice was suddenly uncertain. 'That was why I came.'

So once more Kirsty entered the Woongarra hospital. Kirsty had left Reid on the farm, talking to the firemen. One of them was complaining of a stinging eye, so with luck, Kirsty thought, she could see Bob Henderson and leave before Reid arrived.

Bob Henderson had just finished his hospital breakfast. He pushed away his cup of tea as Kirsty walked through the door, and hard, anxious eyes flew up to stare at her.

'Hell,' he said bluntly.

'I know.' Kirsty grimaced. She should be getting used to this by now. 'I'm like Stephanie. How are you, Mr Henderson?'

'Bob,' he growled. 'And it has to be Dr Maine.'

'Kirsty, to you,' she smiled, pulling up a chair.

He stared at her from under craggy eyebrows. What he saw seemed to confuse him further. 'I don't know how you did it,' he said at last. 'High Born behaves for me, but he won't let anyone else near him. And I saw what he did to Fred last night. He's in the next ward with a compound fracture of his arm.'

'Compound. . .' Kirsty winced. 'Poor Fred.'

'Yeah, and High Born knows Fred. So how did he let you near?'

'I like horses,' Kirsty said simply. 'And I guess they know it.'

'You ride?'

'I've ridden in the past.'

Once more that assessing look. He slowly nodded. 'Yeah, you have the look of it.' Then, 'Tell me the worst. . .'

'What worst would you like to know?' Kirsty asked. 'I can tell you that the stables are gutted completely, but you must already know that. I can tell you that your men have made darned sure nothing else is damaged. By the time I'd been there this morning every one of your horses had been caught, checked and rubbed down. You've an efficient team, Mr Henderson. I've rechecked every one of them, and as far as I can see there's no lasting damage.'

'Most of the mares are in foal.'

They would be. The mares wouldn't be owned by Bob, either. Mares were brought to a top stallion such as High Born a month or so before foaling so they could be served almost immediately afterwards. The fact that they were other people's property would make Bob Henderson even more nervous. 'I can see that. It makes it even more remarkable that you've been lucky so far.'

'So far. . .'

'I can't promise you won't get an early birth or two after the shocks of last night,' Kirsty told him. 'But it's unlikely. They're all grazing placidly this morning. In fact, because most of the pregnancies are reasonably well-advanced, you're less likely to have trouble than if it was early on. Mares that suffer stress early in pregnancy are more likely to drop.'

'Yeah, I've been telling myself that.' He grimaced. 'How about Fancy Kate?'

'Fancy Kate has a lateral tear of her hock. It was tricky but your lads—Danny is it, and Ray?—helped me stitch it. She's looking fine. I don't think she knows she damaged it. She regarded my ministrations as a bit of a nuisance.'

'That's great. And. . . And High Born?' There was

no disguising the worry—and the desperate attempt at nonchalance.

'High Born's gorgeous.' Kirsty smiled. 'He has a few bruises from crashing around in his stall, but there's no major damage at all. Nothing that will affect him for any more than a week.'

The farmer lay back on his pillows and his breath came out in a long, low sigh of relief. 'Nothing that'll affect——'

'His virility?' Kirsty grinned. 'No chance. He was eyeing the mares with frustration this morning. Just itching for one to be in season.'

'His virility is the major part of my income.'

'I assumed that,' Kirsty told him gently. 'And he's fine.'

'And now you can stop worrying and get some sleep, Bob Henderson.'

The voice growled from the door and Kirsty swung around to face Reid. Reid had flung a white coat on over his jeans and buttoned his shirt, but he still looked more a farmer than a doctor. He strode forward and unclipped Bob's observation chart from the end of the bed. 'Your blood pressure's still two hundred and ten over a hundred and twenty-five. If you hadn't decided to stop taking your medication you might have been allowed home—but now you can lie on your back and take your medication until we get it down. And the cortisone drip's staying in until you can sing the national anthem without coughing.'

'Standing at attention too?' Bob asked in mock anxiousness, and Reid grinned.

'And saluting the flag,' he agreed. 'Seriously, Bob, your asthma is still a worry and your blood pressure's too high to let you out of here.'

'I bet Doc Maine here's just lowered it a few points with her news,' Bob said happily. 'But. . . Look, Doc, I gotta get home. I've new stables to build.'

'You're insured?'

'Yeah. . .'

'Well, we'll supply pen and paper and you can lie in bed and plan all you like,' Reid told him. 'If you're insured you can afford a draftsman and builders. There's a phone by your bed. Immediately after your morning sleep you can start work.'

Bob grimaced. 'You really reckon I should stay?'

'You'd be a fool if you didn't,' Reid said bluntly.

Bob hesitated. He looked across at Kirsty. 'You'll keep an eye on my horses?'

'I'll do that.'

'I don't like them being out in the open. . .'

'Short-term they're fine. None of them look as if they're due to drop just yet.'

Bob sighed. 'OK. I'll stay,' he said ungraciously, and then grinned. 'Yeah, all right. I'm grateful to the pair of you. And Dr Maine. . .Kirsty?'

Kirsty raised her eyebrows.

'I've been using Bega vets for the past twenty years. Been paying a fortune in travelling expenses for them to drive over here. I reckon. . .I reckon it might be time to change. If you'd consider being stud vet. . .'

Kirsty took a deep breath.

'Yes, please,' she said.

Two minutes later Kirsty left Reid to his patients and walked slowly back to the hospital entrance. Her tired mind was whirling.

For some reason Bob Henderson's stud-farm hadn't used the previous Woongarra vet, and the income she had anticipated hadn't included being treating veterinarian of a major horse-stud. If it had, then the cost of the practice would have been way out of her price-range. A horse-stud. . .

'Wow,' she said happily to herself. 'Wow!'

'Wow?'

Kirsty jumped a foot. When she came down to earth she found Reid Haslett eyeing her indulgently from the top step.

'You scared me,' she said crossly, and he grinned.

'You don't scare, Dr Maine,' he corrected her. 'I'm

beginning to know that. Kirsty. . .'

'Yes?' Her voice was suddenly breathless.

'Can I take you to dinner tonight?'

Kirsty stared up at him for a long moment. He was wrong. She was scared stiff.

'No,' she said finally—abruptly. 'I have too much work to do—and I'm looking forward to bed.'

It was the last time Kirsty saw Reid for almost two days. She almost managed to put him to the back of her mind. Almost. . .

The days settled down to steady, constant work. Anthea came home from hospital on Thursday, and on Friday presented herself for work. Horrified, Kirsty sent her home, but Anthea reappeared later in the afternoon.

'Just for a couple of hours?' she pleaded. 'So I can tell myself all weekend I've started work.'

Kirsty grinned and relented, and to her delight found that Anthea was quick and willing.

'We work well as a team.' Kirsty smiled as they worked together to remove a fine grass seed from a young schnauzer's ear. It was a procedure that Kirsty hated using general anaesthetic for, yet she needed a competent person to hold the dog still. The boisterous Harley's owner was too squeamish for the job.

'I love it.' Anthea smiled happily back. She looked down as the forceps produced the wax-coated sliver of grass. 'Oh, well done. He'll be happier with that out.'

'He sure will be.' Kirsty patted the young dog's gleaming coat. Harley shook his head, his eyes expressing disbelief that the pain had gone so swiftly. 'But I think your owner is going to have to get you clipped, Harley, mate. Otherwise we'll have you back next week. Either that or keep you confined to a manicured back garden.' She glanced up at Anthea. 'Is Harley the last?'

'He is.' Anthea grinned. 'Your week's work is almost finished, Dr Maine. There's only Saturday morning, and that should be light.' She hesitated. 'I'm coming in, too. Try and stop me. And. . .and do you still want Eve to come in?'

'I sure do.'

'I just thought. . . Well, you're employing me now.'

'Are you saying I should sack your daughter and let you sweep?' Kirsty asked with mock incredulity, and Anthea threw her hands up in mock horror.

'Heaven forbid.'

Anthea left five minutes later. With relief Kirsty started to lock up. Just as she was about to walk out, however, an ancient truck rattled up the headland.

More work. Kirsty stifled a sigh of frustration as a man emerged from the cabin of the truck. He was carrying a dog.

The man looked familiar. Kirsty held the door wide as the man brought the dog into the surgery and frowned. Where had she seen him before?

'Tom Harsham,' the man said roughly. He paused to cough, a dry, hacking cough that made him seem older than he was. 'I've come to get my dog put down.'

Tom Harsham. . . Kirsty didn't recognise the name but she did recognise the voice.

'I've met you before,' she said softly, her eyes on the dog. 'You rescued me the night I arrived in Woongarra.'

'Rescued. . .' The man stared, and then his face broke into a flash of recognition. He cleared his throat and coughed again. 'Damned cold,' he said, as an attempt at an apology. Then, 'You were the girl in the car. . .'

'Stuck in the middle of nowhere,' Kirsty agreed. 'If it wasn't for you I might still be there.'

The man looked away. No comment. It was as if he was ashamed. . .

The dog in his arms gave a slight whimper and Kirsty motioned the big man to lay him on the examination-table.

'What's the problem?' she said. The man's distress

might account for his curious reaction to her.

'I want him put down.'

Kirsty looked down at the limp figure of the Border Collie. He wasn't an old dog, but that he was ill almost to death Kirsty didn't doubt. He lay limp and lifeless.

She looked back up to his owner. Tom Harsham sounded abrupt, cold and uninterested, and if Kirsty hadn't seen the fierce clenching of his fingers she would have thought he didn't care.

'He was run over by a car a year back and suffered kidney damage,' Tom Harsham told her. 'I thought he was OK. . . The old vet said he'd be right, but he's not. He's been getting sicker for two days and now he's dragging his hind legs. It's not right to drag this out. I don't want any operations. No fancy tests and interference. Just. . . Just do—— Look, I've got a sick kid at home. I've got to go.' He laid a fleeting hand on the dog's head. 'Hey, Blacky. . .' he whispered, and he walked out of the surgery. As he hit the cool night air he started coughing again.

Kirsty stared after him. There was something wrong with the man. . .

The man's health wasn't her concern. She had to worry about the dog.

Tom Harsham thought it was kidney failure.

It would be easy enough to put the dog down, but if Kirsty had a weakness it was for Border Collies. Besides, Tom Harsham was obviously fond of his dog. If she could find some other cause. . .

There was nothing. Kirsty took her time to make a thorough examination. The dog was about eight years old, with the fine intelligent eyes of his breed. His legs had given out completely and the dog's breathing was starting to sound laboured as well.

The signs of kidney failure were there all right. Kirsty put her stethoscope above the dog's heart and listened. It wasn't just kidneys now. The heart was beginning to sound erratic.

Kirsty stared down at the file she'd pulled out and

laid on the table. Blacky Harsham. . . Hit by car: rup-
tured spleen, fractured rear leg, kidney failure. . .
Lucky to be alive with that load of injuries. But he'd
recovered. The file said he'd been checked just before
the last vet had left and there was full recovery.

He wasn't recovered now. He was sick almost
to death.

'And your owner's right, old mate,' Kirsty said sadly
as she ran her hand through the dog's thick coat. To
operate on a damaged kidney was risky with the dog
already this sick. Blacky had obviously been through
a terrible time after his collision with the car. It was
the owner's right to ask that he not suffer any longer.

'I just wish I knew. . .' Kirsty stared down at the
dog, wishing she had X-ray eyes. If only X-rays showed
internal organs. . .

An ultrasound might, she thought longingly, her
mind going back to the state-of-the-art veterinary hospital at the zoo. Still. . . No fancy tests, Tom Harsham
had decreed, so even if she were there. . .

Darn! It was a rotten way to end the week—to have
to put a dog down. . .

'Working late, Dr Maine?'

Once again Reid's voice made Kirsty jump. She
should be getting used to it, she thought crossly as her
heart slowed its sudden pumping. Dratted male. . .

'Yes, I'm working late,' she said grimly. 'What does
it look like?'

Reid crossed to the table and looked down at the
limp dog beneath her hands. He whistled soundlessly.
'Not working on a winner here, Kirsty.' His voice had
gentled and Kirsty flinched.

'No.'

'What's wrong?'

'I don't know,' Kirsty admitted. 'I suspect kidney
failure. He damaged his kidneys a year ago in a car
accident.'

'You'll operate?'

'The owner doesn't want me to.' Kirsty put her hand

on the dog's muzzle and gently caressed. The dog
looked up trustingly, his huge brown eyes pain-filled
and weary. 'And his breathing's shallow already. His
heart-rate's erratic.'

Reid frowned. He looked down at the dog. 'This is
the Harsham dog?'

'Yes.'

'I thought I recognised him.' Reid grimaced. 'He
used to be a terror—chased every car in the neighbour-
hood until he was finally hit last year.' He frowned
again. 'He recovered well. The only thing it seemed
to have stopped him doing was chasing cars. I saw him
a few days ago when I was doing a house-call up near
the Harsham place. He was tearing after a rather large
tom-cat as if his pride depended on it. I would have
said there was nothing wrong with him.'

'It's been fast, all right,' Kirsty said.

'Tom Harsham wouldn't have brought him in until
the last minute. He doesn't believe in vets—or doctors
either, for that matter.'

Kirsty looked up. 'He said he had a sick child.'

'Well, what's the bet I won't see it until it's an emergency? Mary Harsham will be home applying hot
poultices and herb tea. . .' Reid frowned again, his
attention once more on the dog. 'Did Tom say how
Blacky got sick?'

'Just general lethargy. Moped about, didn't eat, then
went weak in the back legs. . .'

'Weak. . .' Reid stared. 'You know, Dr Maine,
you're describing the classic symptoms of an animal
with a paralysis tick.'

'A tick. . .?'

'We have a nasty local tick,' Reid told her. 'It's not
common, but in a few areas of scrub around here it's
been known to latch on to victims. It causes gradual
paralysis, breathing problems and death. I haven't seen
a case for a couple of years—but we've had a warm,
wet winter. . .'

'Tick. . . Oh, my. . .' Kirsty's hands were already

parting the dog's coat. 'Of course. I should have thought. . . Of all the stupid. . .' She looked up, her fingers starting to work their way carefully over the dog's hide, searching for a tiny raised welt denoting the presence of a tick. 'It could be. . .'

'It probably is.' Reid was reinforcing what Kirsty already knew—what hadn't made sense. A dog with kidney failure would normally show signs of ill-health before becoming this ill.

'There's an antitoxin.' Kirsty's mind was racing.

'Yes. But it'd take a day to get it here. This dog's too sick for that. There's only one thing we can do, Kirsty Maine. We find this damned tick.'

'But it mightn't be——'

'You're right. It mightn't be a tick. But it's the obvious cause. And the first rule of medicine is to exclude the obvious before doing anything drastic. Like putting patients down. . .'

'They didn't teach you that at medical school.' Kirsty grinned suddenly. 'Putting down *your* patients might not be considered a second option—unless the law's changed since I last read the statute books. Look, Reid, even if we find the tick. . .'

'It's not too late. Recovery's almost miraculous. Antitoxin if the tick can't be found, but we've run out of time for that.'

They worked solidly for an hour. Kirsty didn't ask what Reid had come for. At the back of her mind she wondered whether she should refuse his help, but finding the cause of the dog's problems seemed more important than her personal preferences. Reid was willing to search, and four eyes searching were infinitely preferable to two.

A tiny black spot on a black and white dog. . . It should be easy, Kirsty thought miserably. There should be a swelling. They searched, and as they did the dog grew weaker beneath their hands.

'This is hopeless,' Kirsty whispered as they started over the dog for the third time, searching every infinitesimal space. 'It must be an internal problem.'

'Keep looking.'

'I could just ring for the antitoxin.'

'Keep looking.' Reid's hands paused. He lifted the dog's face. 'I don't suppose. . .' And then, 'Yes. . .' Reid's voice was suddenly a murmur, holding almost unbelieving hope. 'Yes!'

Kirsty had been searching the long line of bushy black tail. Now she looked up to where Reid was staring intently into the dog's face.

'We've got him, Kirsty,' he said triumphantly. 'Just inside the left nostril. You can't see, but there's a welt. I'm sure it's raised. It has to be the damned thing. What we need now is some tweezers.'

And a moment later a defunct tick was lying harmlessly on a swab plate.

Kirsty stared down at the insect, no bigger than a flea. For such a small animal to do that much damage. . .

'Are we too late?' she whispered.

'He'll be fine, I reckon,' Reid grinned. He ruffled the dog's head. 'He's still breathing unaided. What's the bet he'll be beginning to feel better within an hour?'

'As fast as that?'

'I've taken a tick off a local dog before. With him it was as fast as that.'

'I've read of it,' Kirsty said doubtfully. 'But I've never seen it. I'll believe it when I see it.'

'Oh ye of little faith.'

And beneath Reid's hands the dog stirred. He hadn't raised a protest as Kirsty's hands had skilfully extracted the tick. Now the dog's eyes widened. He looked up and his tail gave an almost imperceptible wag.

'What did I tell you?' Reid's grin was enveloping his face, and Kirsty's smile was suddenly as wide. It was rare in medicine to orchestrate a cure like this. It was almost their own, personal miracle.

She carried Blacky over to a readied cage. As she

lowered him in, the dog stretched out to his water bowl and made an unsteady attempt to lap. Kirsty held him so he could touch the water. Three laps later he was exhausted. His legs wouldn't hold him. She laid him gently on the soft bedding and turned back to Reid.

'I'll ring his owner,' she said happily. 'Thank you, Reid.'

'Think nothing of it,' he said softly. He came towards her and lifted her white coat from her shoulders. 'And, after you do that, what about dinner?'

'I. . .I guess. . .' She shouldn't. Kirsty fought for resolve. Anthea and Eve were taking Anthea's mother home and staying there for dinner so she had the kitchen to herself. She should go home, cook herself something simple and go to bed.

She should. . . Instead she looked up at Dr Reid Haslett's face and just knew she was about to do something foolish. 'I'd like dinner,' she managed.

He smiled then, and his smile was as unsure as hers, as though he was doing something just as foolish.

'Make the phone call then, Kirsty,' he said gently. 'And, Kirsty?'

'Yes.'

'I promise you're not on the menu.'

'I. . .I beg your pardon.'

'I won't eat you. You don't have to look so darned scared.'

Tom Harsham was delighted but preoccupied when Kirsty telephoned. 'Hey, that's great,' he told her. 'And it makes sense. The kid took Blacky out rabbiting in the coastal scrub a couple of days back. He'll have picked it up there. You really reckon he'll recover?'

Kirsty looked over to where the dog was sleeping, his chest rising in deep, regular motion. 'I'm almost sure of it. The only thing that could happen now is that his heart gives out, and it's unlikely in an otherwise fit dog.'

'That's great,' he repeated. Kirsty could hear his satisfaction. Then, 'Doctor. . .?'

'Yes.'

'Do you think. . .? Would you mind hanging on to him for me overnight? I. . . The wife and I are a bit busy. I can pick him up tomorrow morning.'

'That's fine,' Kirsty told him, inwardly sighing. As she'd said, the only repercussion she feared now was heart trouble, and he'd be less stressed in his own kennel. It meant she would have to come back here tonight to check on him. Still. . . Reid might come too. . .

She hung up and turned to her dinner date.

'All done?' he asked, and smiled.

And Kirsty's heart did a back-flip.

She wasn't ready at all. She never would be. Not for this.

'I need to wait for a little. . . Just to make sure he is on the road to recovery and we haven't missed another tick.'

'That's OK.' He smiled his heart-stopping smile. 'I'll go back to the hospital and do an hour's medico-legal reports. If I come to Anthea's house then, will you be ready?'

There was a long silence before Kirsty finally spoke.

'I'll be ready,' she said.

CHAPTER EIGHT

SOMETHING wasn't right.

Kirsty had driven her car back home and arrived almost at the same time as Reid. She showered swiftly and changed from her work jeans into a simple cotton dress for the evening. 'You don't need to change,' Reid had told her, his eyes appreciating her slim form in her work jeans and checked shirt.

She did, though. She had been handling sick and injured animals all day and Reid had understood.

'I feel the same,' he had conceded. 'By the time I've inspected putrid throats, assorted chicken pox and infected toes of forty patients or more I start to feel pretty darned unclean.'

It was almost worth it to change. Kirsty came downstairs in a pale green dress, its yielding folds accentuating her figure, and Reid's eyes told her it *was* worth it. She had opted for a mid-calf-length dress, but its neckline was too low. Dangerous thought. . .

'A night out,' Reid said slowly, his eyes moving over Kirsty's slim form. 'How long since I've done this?'

It was probably longer since Kirsty had done it, she thought fearfully. And even now. . . Even now she thought she was probably a fool.

It wasn't just Reid's presence that was making her uncomfortable. Something was sitting obstinately in the back of her mind. Something she should remember. It was like knowing the date was someone's birthday— someone who would be hurt if she forgot—but she couldn't remember who. Something she should know. . .

Reid ushered her into the town's only decent restaurant, but Kirsty was only half aware of her surroundings. Something. . .

Chez Nous was rather ostentatiously named for a good Australian restaurant. It had crêpes on the menu for dessert, but that was its only claim to French cooking. Kirsty chose a simple lobster salad, and when it came it was delicious.

It could have been magic. If Kirsty had been six years younger. . . If Neil or Stephanie had never happened. . . If Reid was one whit less handsome and didn't make her catch her breath every time she looked up at him. . . And if the thing niggling at the back of her mind would only surface. . .

'What's wrong?' Reid asked as the remains of their main course were cleared. He had eaten slowly and said little as he watched the girl before him, soaking in her unconscious loveliness and the atmosphere of the night around him. Chez Nous was set in the harbour, and the town's fishing-fleet was anchored outside the plate-glass windows.

The harbour lights reflected on the still waters of the sea, and to the east a sliver of silver moon was just rising. A magic night. . .

'I don't know. Something. . .' Kirsty took a sip of her wine and pushed it away. She was trying to think and it wasn't helping. Reid wasn't helping.

'Something you've forgotten?' Reid's eyes were understanding. One medical professional to another— he knew how disastrous the consequences of forgetting could be.

'No. I don't. . .' Kirsty shook her head. 'Something's wrong. I don't know. . .' And then her eyes widened. 'Yes, I do.'

He waited. This was a strange dinner-date, to sit with a woman whose mind was elsewhere—who was trying not to think of him, trying to block his presence as she put her hands to her eyes and clenched her fingers.

'Tom Harsham. . .'

'Yes?'

'He said he had a sick child.'

Reid carefully put his wine back on the table. 'And?' he said slowly.

'When I rang to tell him Blacky would live, he told me his son had taken Blacky into the scrub rabbiting a couple of days ago. And Blacky got a tick and became ill. And Tom Harsham's child is ill. I wonder. . .I wonder if it's the same child?'

Reid was already rising, his hand beckoning the waiter for the bill.

'I might be wrong,' Kirsty said hesitantly. 'Tom had a cough himself, and I don't suppose a paralysis tick causes coughing. It's probably just a cold going through the whole family. . .'

'We can't afford not to check, can we, Dr Maine?' Reid had flipped back to his cool, professional self. 'Even if it's not the same child. I should have made the connection. You told me the child was ill.'

'But he must be only just starting to show symptoms. Surely they'd have brought him to you if they were worried?'

'You don't know the Harshams,' Reid said grimly. 'They had home births without any medical help at all. They've refused to get the children vaccinated. Tom Harsham keeps his family almost fiercely apart. They brought Blacky to the vet when he was run over because his leg had to be set and they couldn't do it. This time they thought he needed to be put down and Tom Harsham's too attached to his dog to do it.'

'Then we should telephone.'

'No. If I telephoned, Tom Harsham would in all probability tell me to go to the devil. I want to see that child, and I want to see him before they bring him to me because he's gone into respiratory failure. We'll pretend we're doing the guy a favour and bringing his dog home. That should make him grateful enough to get us in the front door.'

The waiter appeared smoothly, professionally, by Reid's side. He looked from Kirsty to Reid in concern. Obviously he knew who his customers were and he was anxious as to the outcome of the evening. 'Is something wrong?'

'The food was great,' Reid reassured him. 'But duty calls.'

'Duty didn't even telephone,' the waiter said wryly. 'Do you guys just sit over meals and dream up work? I wish I could do that. I'd have a few more customers in my restaurant.'

The Harshams lived five miles out of town, and by the time they arrived Kirsty had talked herself into believing they were overreacting. She sat silently beside Reid with the fast-recovering Blacky on her knee. Blacky was content to lie placidly on her lap, but when they'd returned to the surgery he'd stood to greet them. The dog had recovered enough to go home, Kirsty conceded, especially as it would give Reid the excuse he needed to approach the Harshams.

She was still almost certain that her fears were groundless, though. Tom Harsham's cough made her almost sure. Almost. . .

'So we're on a wild-goose chase.' Reid was concentrating on the bumpy track as she voiced her thoughts. 'It's a lovely night for a goose chase, though. So why not sit back and enjoy it?'

The Harshams' house was set well back from the road, surrounded by overgrown garden, derelict fences and old car bodies.

'Tom runs a junk business on the side,' Reid told Kirsty, seeing her look of distaste.

Kirsty might have been dismayed, but Blacky was anything but. He sat up as they pulled up at the house and as Kirsty opened the door he struggled to be put down. By the time Reid knocked on the door Blacky was standing unaided, his tongue panting joyfully, waiting to be let in. Home!

Mary Harsham didn't even see him. She opened the door, took one look at Reid, and burst into tears.

'Oh, Doctor. Oh, thank God you've come. I was

just about to make Tom bring Benjamin in to see you.'

Tom Harsham appeared behind his wife. His eye-brows hit his hairline when he saw who was at the door.

'We've brought Blacky back, Mr Harsham——' Kirsty began but got no further. Tom Harsham had grabbed Reid by the arm and was practically dragging him through the house.

The child was lying limply on piled bedclothes on the settee in the main living-room. The signs of a child not feeling well were obvious. Among and beside the bedclothes were a scrap-book, a packet of colouring pencils, a couple of comics and a half-drunk glass of orange juice. The books and comics, Kirsty noticed, were still in a neat pile, and her impression of serious illness deepened. Paediatric medicine was very like veterinary medicine, she had been told, and she believed it. When children were ill, they acted ill. Healthy children who'd managed to con their parents into allowing a day off school didn't usually waste the opportunity by sleeping.

Reid crossed swiftly to the sofa and stooped over the wan child. He lifted the little boy's wrist.

'Hi, Benjamin,' he said gently. 'They tell me you're crook. Want to tell me about it yourself?'

The boy raised fearful eyes to Reid. He looked about eight. He was very much a miniature version of his father, but where his father was almost bald and his skin was weathered, Benjamin had downy, white-blond hair and fair skin. His eyes were enormous in his white face.

'I can't walk,' he whispered. 'I've been sick. Mum thought I was just getting Dad's cold. But now I can't move my legs. . .'

'It's just happened,' Mary Harsham gulped behind them. 'And I gave him a drink of orange juice and he couldn't hold it. He said his arms felt funny. . .'

Reid nodded. 'And your dog had a paralysis tick.' Reid replaced the boy's wrist on the bedclothes. 'It sounds like you have too, Benjamin.'

'We thought of it,' Tom Harsham growled. He paused, racked by a spasm of coughing. 'This bloody cold,' he finally managed. 'Sorry, Doc. Of course we thought of a tick, though. We're not bloody fools.'

'I never said you were.' Obviously an undercurrent of tension ran between Reid and Harsham from previous encounters. 'But, despite the fact that you have a cold, nothing else but a tick makes sense. The medical conditions causing paralysis are rare. We can't rule out polio because of your refusal to vaccinate, but seeing Blacky——'

'Polio. . .' Mary Harsham turned as deathly white as her son. 'Polio!' She turned on her husband. 'You bloody fool,' she flung at him. 'If Ben's got polio. . .'

Reid stood and took Mrs Harsham's hands. 'Don't panic, Mary,' he said firmly. 'There's no need. The chances of Ben having polio are almost nil. If Blacky hadn't had the tick I'd be forced to check, but the evidence is that the dog had the tick, and he got it when he went with Ben into the scrub, so there must be another tick.'

'But we've looked,' Mary moaned.

'Well, let's look again.' Reid's black bag, innocuously carried in by his side, was placed on the floor. He sat down on the settee and produced his stethoscope.

'You came because of Ben,' Tom gasped, staring down at the bag. 'You came bloody well prepared.'

'Dr Maine told me her concerns when she heard Ben was ill,' Reid said briefly, and turned back to Ben. His face closed in concentration as he lifted Ben's pyjama-top and listened.

'Of all the nerve. . .' Tom wheeled on Kirsty. 'I'll thank you for keeping out of our business.'

'You'll thank Dr Maine for bringing us Dr Haslett,' his wife snapped. 'Oh, for goodness' sake, Tom, just shut up. I've had enough of your bluster. You're as scared about Ben as I am and we're lucky Dr Haslett's here.' She knelt down beside her little boy. Reid was folding away his stethoscope. 'What. . .what do we do?'

'There's no sign of breathing problems yet,' Reid told her. 'I'll have a fast look here but if we can't find what we're looking for we'll take him straight into hospital and keep looking there until the air ambulance arrives to take him to Melbourne. I'll telephone Melbourne and ask for a flight now.'

'Air ambulance. . .' Mary Harsham was white with fear. 'Melbourne. . .'

Reid nodded. 'I'm being over-cautious,' he told her. 'But Melbourne's where the antitoxin is. The flight either has to bring the antitoxin to us or take Ben to the antitoxin, and the second way's safest. When we find this tick the chances are that Ben will recover immediately, but because the signs of paralysis are starting there's a chance it could affect his heart. The Children's Hospital has a far more extensively equipped Intensive Care Unit than I have. They'll probably send him home in twenty-four hours, Mary, but I'd be taking a risk by not sending him.' He looked up at Tom Harsham. 'You don't want me to take that risk, do you, Tom?'

Tom closed his eyes in a gesture of defeat. Do your worst, his slumped shoulders said.

Kirsty nodded silently. There was a chance Blacky's heart could be affected too, but the risk to a dog didn't warrant air ambulances. The risk to a small boy, though. . . Well, Reid was right. He had to go. If only they could find the tick before the flight. . .

'Do you have any itchy or sore spots at all?' Reid asked the child. 'Anything, Ben? Something that feels like a mosquito bite? Something that just feels a bit lumpy or funny?'

The child shook his head. 'I can't feel my legs very well,' he confessed. 'Or my hands. They sort of feel numb. . .'

'OK. Well, how about your dad and mum and I having a really good look now?' Reid asked him. 'An all-over body-search. You can pretend you're the good guy in a western being searched for concealed weapons.'

'Pretty funny weapon.' Ben tried to smile, but it didn't quite come off.

'It'd be a good way to put a villain out of action.' Reid grinned in agreement. 'Stick your hands up or I'll let my tick out of his jar!'

The child gave a watery chuckle.

'I'll take Blacky outside,' Kirsty offered, knowing instinctively that she wasn't wanted. An eight-year-old boy was old enough to have his pride. Mum and Dad searching his body might be OK, and maybe even the doctor, but the lady vet shouldn't see him in such an undignified position.

Reid nodded at her and she knew she'd done the right thing.

Blacky was ready for bed. The dog was lying by the back door when Kirsty went to find him, waiting patiently to be released. Kirsty opened the door and the dog staggered uncertainly out into the night.

There was a dog kennel out by one of the sheds. Luckily the moon was huge, and Kirsty could see clearly where the dog was headed. She followed him, gave him a farewell pat on his head and stooped to make sure he'd settled for the night. The dog's head went down on his paws and he was asleep in seconds. It was obviously blessedly good to be home.

He needed water. Kirsty picked up the water dish lying by the kennel and checked it, but it was close to empty. She walked along the row of shedding and then stopped as curiosity got the better of her. From one of the sheds came a muffled squawking and clattering. It sounded like an aviary where the birds were being troubled by something. At this time of night birds were usually well-roosted—but something was disturbing this lot.

A water tap was just near the shed door. Kirsty filled Blacky's water dish, took it back to him, and then went round the other side of the sheds to where she'd heard the noise.

She'd expected the wire netting of an aviary. The birds she could hear weren't chooks. There were the sounds of birds flying, and a couple of thuds denoting a bird that had hit the wooden wall.

It was probably just a rat on the floor of their cage after grain that was disturbing them, Kirsty thought, but where was the front of the aviary? It certainly wasn't a cleverly designed modern aviary, with boards that covered the screening at night. The shed was ancient.

She stood, listening for a while, reluctant to go and disturb Tom Harsham for what was probably nothing. A rat would do little harm unless the birds were nesting, and even then a correctly designed aviary would have nesting-boxes high enough to deter small predators.

'Kirsty!'

Kirsty swung around to the house. A beam of light was thrown from the back door, and Reid's form was black against it.

'I'm taking Ben down to the hospital. We can't find it.'

Kirsty came over to him. 'No luck?'

'Not yet, and I've decided I'm wasting time here because the light's not good. I've rung Melbourne. The air ambulance is at Bega, so it'll be here in half an hour. They had a car crash there this afternoon—someone with a major spinal injury—but the patient died before the plane arrived. They were just about to return to Melbourne when I rang. It means there's medical staff aboard and ready, and I want to search Ben thoroughly before the flight. Will you drive while I hold him in the back seat?'

'Sure.' Kirsty came quickly, knowing Reid's reluctance to leave a child as sick as Ben untended. Ben didn't have breathing problems yet, but the paralysis was widespread and trouble could start fast.

Two minutes later they had the child safely stowed with Reid in the back of his car. Mary Harsham was coming too. She sat rigidly in the front passenger seat, an overnight bag clutched on her lap as she stared straight ahead. Her fear was almost palpable. Tom Harsham stood beside the car as Kirsty started the engine. He was forced to stay because of the other children asleep in the house, but he clearly didn't like it.

'We'll let you know as soon as anything changes, Tom,' Reid promised. 'Let's go, Kirsty.'

Kirsty looked sympathetically up at the burly man beside the car. His was the hardest role. To wait. . .

'Maybe you could check your birds while you wait,' she suggested. 'While I was putting Blacky to bed I heard something disturbing them.'

'Birds. . .' The man took a step back from the car. There was a moment of complete silence. Then, 'I don't have any birds,' he said flatly.

'Kirsty, let's move it,' Reid said roughly from the back seat. 'We're wasting time.'

Kirsty was getting accustomed to the back-roads of the district by now, her sense of direction growing surer. She drove swiftly and was soon pulling up outside the brightly lit Casualty entrance.

Was it her imagination or was Ben growing weaker? He tried to put his hand out for his mother as Reid lifted him from the car. The arm lifted maybe two inches and fell uselessly back. The little boy gave a sob of hopelessness.

'I can't move,' he whimpered.

Kirsty was staring at the hand as if struck. 'Reid. . .'

'Let's get a stretcher,' Reid snapped. 'Kirsty, will you——?'

'Reid, stop.'

He turned and stared at her. 'For heaven's sake. . .' A nurse was coming through the Casualty entrance, her face an enquiry. Reid started to walk but Kirsty reached out and took Ben's small hand in hers. Oblivi-

ous of Reid's impatience she held the small hand up
to the brilliant light illuminating the ambulance entry.

Beneath each nail was a line of black grime—the
grime of a child who'd played outside and then become
ill quickly. He hadn't been washed. . .

'Ten to one that's where we'll find it,' she breathed.
On Ben's white skin with his white hair nothing else
made sense.

Reid stared down at the hand, then across to Kirsty.
His face lit. 'It'd be too big,' he said doubtfully.

'It doesn't have to be very big to cause such damage.'
Kirsty took a deep breath. 'Let's clean his fingernails
and see.'

'Right.' Reid looked around to the nurse. 'We need a
stretcher trolley, please, Sister. We'll take Ben straight
through to Theatre. The light's better there.'

'A procedure?' the nurse asked tentatively.

Reid smiled and shook his head. 'I hope not, Sister.'
He grinned down at the boy in his arms. 'With luck
we've just brought young Ben Harsham in for a
manicure.'

And that was all it was. The tick was smaller than
the one they had taken from Blacky—no bigger than
a pin-head—but after Reid had carefully scraped dirt
from under each fingernail the body of the tick stayed
where it was. It looked like a spot of dirt, but it was
immovable.

Kirsty had hesitated as Reid and the nurse wheeled
Ben into Theatre. This wasn't her job. Reid, though,
had smiled up at her as he waited for the nurse to
open the theatre doors.

'I believe you bet at odds of ten to one, Dr Maine,'
he had said. 'A risky business. I assume you're interested in the outcome of your bet?' Then, as the dirt
had come away and left the tiny speck in place, he
had flashed her a look of pure triumph. 'Nice work,
Dr Maine.'

Kirsty smiled. 'We must be in the wrong pro-
fessions,' she said happily. 'My patient needed a doctor

and your Ben needed the vet.' She stared down at the tick, hardly able to believe it could really be this easy.

'Will you kill it?'

'I'll pare the nail down a couple of millimetres,' Reid told her. 'I don't want to risk the thing breaking if I drag it out from under.' He smiled down at the child and held the offending hand up for him to see. 'There's the cause of the trouble, Ben. We'll take this little trouble-maker off, check to make sure you don't have any more of the pests, and with luck you'll have your legs by morning.'

Ben stared up from the theatre table, clearly still very scared and totally unconvinced. 'My legs feel. . . they feel like they've gone forever.'

'They'll be back.' Reid smiled. 'I promise.' Reid turned to the nurse by his side. 'I want a local anaes-thetic—a finger-block.' He turned back to Ben. 'I know your finger's almost numb anyway, but I'll put a little more anaesthetic in to make sure you won't feel what I'm doing.' He pointed to the nail. 'I'll cut your fingernail really, really short—so short we'll have to pop a bandage on later, because the skin will be tender. I want to get this pest off in one piece. If I just pull what I can reach of him, I risk leaving half of him under your skin. If that happens, you'll still get a little more of his poison and, as well as that, his mess will infect your finger. Do you agree?'

It was a polished approach. The small boy gave Reid's proposal careful thought and then nodded. 'I agree,' he whispered.

The procedure took five minutes. Reid's operating skills were swift and sure, Kirsty noted appreciatively, though she had never doubted they would be. The man was good. . .

'You really think a lot of him, don't you?' she remembered saying to Anthea—goodness, was it less than a week ago?

'The whole town does,' Anthea had replied. 'I guess, in time, you will too.'

She looked at him now, his face fierce with concentration as he dressed the small finger, and then softening as he looked up to share a reassuring joke with his small patient. A caring, compassionate man. . .

She was falling in love. . .

Falling. . . Kirsty had heard the term before but it had never made sense. Falling. . .

Now, though. . . The sensation she was feeling was just that. Falling. Her solid ground had been cut away and she was in free-fall, with no control of where she was or where she was going. Reid finished the dressing, ruffled Ben's blond hair, and turned with a smile to Kirsty, and Kirsty's free-fall turned into a slow spin.

It was as much as she could do not to put out a hand to save herself. Reid would have taken it if she had. He was coming towards her now, his smile fading in concern.

'Are you all right, Dr Maine?'

She made a huge effort. 'Of course. . . Of course I'm OK,' she managed. 'I don't faint at the sight of a little blood.'

'That's nice to know,' he said drily. He turned to Mary Harsham, who had been silently watching all this time. 'Mary, Ben's going to be fine, I'm sure. We'll still send him to Melbourne, though, if it's OK with you. I don't want to take any chances. With luck, they'll bring you back by road ambulance in twenty-four hours.'

'That's fine by me,' Mary said, her voice trembling with relief and a hint of defiance. 'Though what Tom will say now that you've found the tick. . .'

'I'll settle it with Tom,' Reid told her. 'You'll go with Ben?'

'I'd like that. But——'

'No buts.' Reid smiled. 'I said I'll settle it with Tom, and I will.' He turned and his slow, heart-stopping smile drifted over Kirsty like a shaft of soft white light. Then he smiled back at Mary. 'Dr Maine and I were in the midst of our very first date when Ben's tick came between us. So, as soon as we see you and Ben safely on to the plane, we'll continue our date by driving back out to your place, placating Tom, and then driving back by the coast road. Can you think of any better way to spend our first date?'

Mary looked from Kirsty to Reid and back again. She must be seeing Kirsty's blush, Kirsty thought desperately. Her face was burning.

'It's the way it's done hereabouts,' Mary said softly, as though reassuring the young vet. 'It's the way my Tom started courting me. On the coast road. . .'

It was a fast drive back to Tom Harsham's. Kirsty had demurred as they watched the lights of the small plane disappear into the night sky, but Reid had brushed aside her protests.

'If I telephone Tom he won't listen,' Reid had explained. 'He's angry and upset, and, despite the façade, he's scared silly. I couldn't calm him before because I was in a rush to get Ben to hospital. Face to face, I can talk to the man. And you promised me a dinner-date, Dr Maine,' he had added softly. 'A promise is a promise, so just pipe down and enjoy it.'

So she had piped down, sitting silently in the passenger seat of Reid's car, but knowing that Reid's order to enjoy was impossible. She wasn't cold, but periodically a tremor went through her body and she hugged her cotton frock tighter to herself. Reid glanced across at her but didn't say a word.

They stopped briefly outside the Harshams'. Whatever protests Tom might have made were privy only to Reid's ears. Kirsty sat in the car and waited.

Waited for what? Another tremor went through her and she brushed a tear angrily from her cheek. Of all the stupid reactions. . . She was behaving like a love-sick teenager. A teenager who was scared to death.

Reid came back to the car and glanced across at Kirsty. He could hardly see her in the dim light, but he must have been able to see enough.

'Kirsty——' he started.

'Just take me home,' Kirsty whispered. 'Please, Reid. I don't. . .I don't like this.'

'Being with me?'

She didn't answer. She couldn't.

Reid glanced at her again and started the engine without a word.

He didn't hurry. The coast road was breathtakingly lovely at this time of night, with the pale moon washing the ocean and the stars brilliant so far from city lights. The few town lights of Woongarra made no imprint on their brilliance. They were shining as though here, at least, they could display their splendour.

Let him take me straight home, Kirsty was pleading silently to herself. Let him. . .

But of course he didn't. A mile from town Reid pulled off the road to a parking bay. The signpost in the moonlight said simply, 'Ocean Views'.

'Reid. . .'

'I'm not going to rape you, Kirsty,' Reid said gently as he pulled the car to a halt. 'But I think we should have this thing out, don't you?'

'This thing. . .?'

'This electricity. . .this. . .call it what you will. Whatever makes you crackle with tension whenever I come near you. Whatever makes me see you even when you aren't near. Whatever makes me want to make you smile more than anything else in the world.'

'Don't. . .'

He rose from the car and came around to her side. Opening the car door, he held out his hand. 'Come and see the stars, Kirsty.'

She rose and went with him. She didn't have a choice. But as they reached the wooden rail forming a safety barrier between them and the drop to the beach, she pulled her hand out of his.

'Is this the standard first-date rendezvous, then?' she said bitterly.

'It's called Lovers' Leap.' Reid smiled. 'Not that anyone's actually leapt. I don't think anyone could stand in such a beautiful spot and contemplate suicide, do you, Kirsty? Especially not lovers.'

'But we're not lovers.' It was a frightened whisper—almost a plea.

'Are we not?' Reid asked slowly. He reached out and took her cold hands between his. 'Are we not, Kirsty? It's true I never thought I could feel like this again. But I do. Therefore I am, I believe, a lover. A lover of Kirsty Maine.'

'A lover of Stephanie. . .'

The words were out before she could stop them. The pain around her heart was threatening to overwhelm her.

Reid didn't pull away, though. He stood, looking down at her in the washed moonlight, and his look was serious and searching.

'You look like a woman I can't think of without cringing,' he said softly. 'And yet I'm falling in love. Not with a face. With a woman. With Kirsty Maine.'

'You can't separate them,' Kirsty whispered. 'It's crazy, Reid. The coincidence. . . It's crazy.'

'It's crazy,' Reid admitted. 'But crazier things have happened.' His hands pulled her closer. '"Ye gods! annihilate but space and time, And make two lovers happy",' he quoted softly. 'And maybe they can, Kirsty. Maybe they have. I don't know what shadow you're under—one day I hope you'll tell me—but whatever it is. . . We can take now and go forward.'

'Reid, I don't think. . .' Kirsty's trembling was increasing to the stage where Reid could feel it. His hands tightened, willing strength into her, but still the fear was there. Dear God, she couldn't. To let herself fall again. To expose herself to the pain all over again. . .

She had already fallen, her heart was saying. And still her head was screaming at her. No! No!

He would have none of her denial. Reid was looking

down at her, his face watching hers as he saw conflicting emotions sweep over her face, over and over. . .

And there was only one way he could do anything about the fear there. There was only one thing his heart told him to do.

He pulled her close, his lean, shadowed face bent over hers, his hand forced her face up to his, and he kissed her.

He had kissed her before. This, though, was different. The times he had touched her before it had almost seemed as though it was the kiss of a man being forced against his will. This was the kiss of a man telling her she was loved. A kiss saying, Open your heart. Trust me. Love me, Kirsty, and let yourself live again in my love. . .

She was lost from the moment his lips touched her. The sound of the sea washed against the rocks beneath them and she was down there in the sea, drowning in the night—drowning in the taste of his lips, the feel of his face against hers, of his arms holding her to his hard, muscled body. Her breasts moulded to his chest as though they were meant to lie there.

Here was her home. Here was her love.

It was like waking from a bad dream. If she could let herself forget. Forget just for now. Forget, and pretend time and tide could be turned.

It was crazy. Impossible. Still her lips parted under Reid's, and her hands lifted almost involuntarily to touch his face. The skin of his chiselled cheeks and jaw was rough. Neil had shaved twice a day. Neil had never felt like that. . .

Reid felt her sudden resistance and released her fractionally from his lips. His eyes asked her a question.

'Whatever it is, Kirsty love, put it away. There's only now. There's only this moment.'

And his hands tightened again and the kiss deepened.

Put it away. . . . Kirsty gave a tiny whimper of resistance, and then she did just that. She let herself go.

She put the pain of the past behind her just for now. She put the pain away just for this magic moment of thinking she was loved—that the awful abyss of loneliness didn't have to go on.

And her mouth kissed him back. Her lips parted and welcomed him into her, savouring the feel of his tongue as he explored the smoothness of her white teeth. She bit down, ever so gently, and he felt the pressure and laughed joyfully deep within. She could feel his laughter.

His hands were sliding down the soft cotton of her dress, feeling the slim contours of her body. They came around to cup her breasts, and her breasts reacted to his touch with exquisite pleasure. When his fingers found the looseness of her low neckline allowed them access, and a hand came down to touch and tease the proudly upright nipples, it was as much as she could do not to weep with pleasure. Dear God, it was so good.

Her thighs were alight with desire and love. Her whole body was aflame. Kirsty's hands were doing an exploration of their own, and she could feel his body's arousal. He wanted her as much as she wanted him.

'Come with me, my love.' Reid's voice was rough with suppressed passion as he released her and gripped her only by her hand. 'I know where we can go. . .'

She was limp in his hold. She watched with suspended thought as he lifted the boot of his car and removed a big rug. She followed where he led, down the rough track to the beach below. His hand held hers and that was all that mattered. And when he spread the rug for her on a secluded section of the little cove, and his hands slowly began to undress her, she made no demur. This was a night out of her life. One crazy night from a future full of loneliness.

'Reid. . .' She wasn't quite crazy. Not totally. Somehow she found the strength to draw back as she fought for sanity. 'Reid, I haven't taken any precautions.'

He unfastened the last button from the bodice of her dress and the soft fabric folds fell to the sand. 'I'm a boy scout from way back.' He smiled down at her. '"Be prepared" is my motto.'

She frowned. 'But how long. . .? I mean, have you often. . .?' She faltered and stopped. There was a stillness around them, broken only by the hushed sounds of foam rushing up and down the sand. Then he bent and kissed her lightly on the lips. It was a kiss of infinite tenderness.

'I haven't often,' he told her. 'I haven't since Stephanie, if you must know. Once bitten. . .'

'So you haven't made love to anyone. . .until Stephanie returned. . .'

Once again, silence. For a moment Kirsty thought there would be anger. She waited, but the anger didn't come. It couldn't on a night like this. A night of warmth and stillness, of beauty and love.

'I'm not making love to Stephanie,' Reid said at last. 'I'm making love to Kirsty Maine, the new woman in my life. New, Kirsty. New and loved. And loved for her own beautiful, clever, caring self. My Kirsty. . .'

She had no armour against him. She couldn't stop the soft, half whispered words and she didn't want to. They filled the aching void in her heart, and she placed her hands up around his neck and drew his head down to her.

'Reid. . .'

'Yes, my love. . .' Her bra was causing him some trouble. The fastenings finally loosened, and he gave a satisfied grunt of pleasure as the wispy garment fell away. Her breasts were white in the moonlight, proud and uplifted. Waiting. . .

'Don't talk, Reid,' Kirsty whispered. 'Just. . . Just love me.'

He drew back and looked down at her, his eyes hooded and strange. Slowly his hands traced her naked skin, down around each breast, down to where the fire was building to a flame she thought could never be doused.

'You are so beautiful. . .'

'Just love me,' she pleaded. 'Please, Reid. . .'

'I can never do anything else,' he told her. With a moan of ecstasy he pulled her down to lie on the thick waiting rug. Full-length they lay against each other. Somehow his clothes too were gone, and they lay skin against skin, the soft night breeze caressing their naked bodies.

This might be a love of one night—a love that couldn't last until morning—but for now Kirsty could ask for no more. She held Reid to her in a fierce and savage hunger, and when the night exploded into passion her world exploded too. She cried out into the night, and her love melted her to a white-hot heat.

But the pain was still there.

Waiting. . .

CHAPTER NINE

THE oasis of happiness was destined to be of short duration. Kirsty lay sated in strong, enfolding arms until an insistent electronic beep sounded from the direction of Reid's discarded clothing. Ruefully he pulled away, read the small illuminated message, and grimaced.

'The world calls, my Kirsty,' he said. He pulled his clothes on and then turned to help her as she fumbled in the moonlight for her dress. 'Just as well, though. The tide's due in soon. We'd float off into the sunrise if we stayed here much longer.'

It sounded OK to Kirsty. To sail off into the sunrise. . . To have this moment forever. . .

But Reid's hands were helping her adjust the buttons of her dress and his hands suggested urgency.

'What is it?' she asked.

'An elderly lady with chest pain,' Reid told her. 'It'll probably turn out to be indigestion, but I daren't risk it. Kirsty. . .?'

'Yes. . .'

He pulled her to her feet. 'Tomorrow you're coming to my mother's for lunch, right?'

'Y-yes,' she whispered uncertainly.

'Good.' He pulled her to him in a hard, possessive kiss. 'Well, until then, my Kirsty. Until then, know that you are loved.'

Kirsty woke, therefore, to her own soft bed in Anthea's house. She had come in, dream-like, showered in a trance and fallen numbly into bed. No trace of sand or anything else from the night remained as she opened her eyes to the morning. It might have been a dream.

'Know that you are loved. . .'

The words whispered in her mind, and she shook her head against the pillows, trying to find some vestige of reality in all that was happening to her.

It had to stop. This was crazy. Reid Haslett was making love to someone who looked like his ex-wife, and Kirsty Maine wasn't free to love—even if she knew she really was loved in return.

She turned bleakly to the dresser. Neil's face smiled gently down at her from the silver frame.

'I won't break my promise,' she whispered. 'Oh, Neil, I won't. . .'

But where could she find the strength to resist Reid? Where had strength been last night? She hadn't any, she acknowledged to herself. Reid had wanted her and she had wanted him just as badly. And his body had made her feel different than she had ever felt before. His body had loved her and assured her she was loved. His body had made her whole. . .

'Which goes to show how much physical need can make me a hypocrite,' she said bitterly into the early morning light, and then broke off as a knock sounded on the bedroom door. 'Come in,' she called cautiously, and pulled her nightgown closer.

Of course it wasn't Reid. Her landlady's small daughter bounced into the bedroom, her bright little budgie perched precariously on the top of her head.

'Custard's due to have his stitches out today,' Eve informed the recumbent Kirsty in a voice that announced this was an event of national significance. 'I thought you might like to take them out early.'

'Like now!' Kirsty glanced at her bedside table. 'Eve Watts, it is appallingly early. I can't possibly be a vet at this hour.'

'Go take a hike,' said Custard.

Kirsty grinned, the confusing emotions of the previous night lifting with the cheerfulness of the pair before her. 'I couldn't agree more, Custard,' she told the yellow budgerigar. 'Go take a hike is my professional opinion exactly.'

Eve was undeterred. Kirsty watched as the child lifted the little bird off her head by encouraging him to move to her finger. She placed the budgie down on Kirsty's coverlet and Custard immediately started pecking at the tiny embroidered roses. He lifted his tail and deposited a nice neat dropping on the whiteness. 'Eve Watts, your mother will have my hide,' Kirsty expostulated. 'Take him away immediately!'

'The droppings don't stain,' Eve said scornfully. 'He did one in my hair last week.'

'Ugh!'

Eve just grinned, then held up a black bag. 'I brought your bag up for you. I thought you'd probably have what you needed in it to take the stitches out.'

'Horrible child.'

There was no help for it. Morning had come. The events of the night before slipped away as if they had been a strange and disturbing dream. A dream that could never be repeated.

At least she still had her work. Her work was currently hopping from embroidered rose to embroidered rose, hoping for something edible among the cotton.

She lifted the little yellow bird with a finger, and then caught him firmly with her free hand. Custard squawked with the indignity. 'Well, I'm glad you're feeling better,' Kirsty told him.

'Go to blazes,' said Custard. 'Take a hike.'

The stitches were still neatly in place. Kirsty slipped out of bed and took the little bird over by the window, where the light was better. Lifting his wing, she examined the healing wound and was satisfied with what she saw. The incision had healed nicely. There was no sign of suppuration—no infection—and the little bird was obviously not pecking at it himself.

'There's pair of surgical scissors in the top of my bag,' she told Eve. She might as well remove the stitches now. There was no getting rid of Eve and her dratted budgie until they were removed.

It was a simple process. Custard, after his initial

protest, had decided the wisest course of action was
to do nothing. He lay placidly in her fingers as she cut
each stitch and lifted it away.

Two minutes later the thread was entirely gone.
Kirsty carefully examined the injured wing. It seemed
to have full motion. Seemed. . .

It was so darned difficult to know. The tiny bird had
nerves so close to the surface, and she'd had to operate
so fast. Five-minute microsurgery, she thought grimly.
Microsurgery without the microscope. Still, at least the
tumour was gone, and even if Custard could no longer
fly he could still have a happy little life.

There was only one way to find out what he was
capable of. She took the bird back over to the big bed,
giving him a soft place to land if the wing didn't func-
tion. She held him a foot above the bed and released
her hand.

Custard didn't fall. With a chirp of delight he lifted,
sensing instinctively that the constricting stitches were
gone. He swooped twice around the full circle of the
room and dived back to land on his favourite place—
Eve's head. There he sat, triumphant in his recovery.
His wings were slightly spreadeagled from the effort,
and he was breathing rapidly after a week of confine-
ment and then unaccustomed activity, but there was
nothing wrong with him. No muscle or nerve damage at all.

It was a moment of immense satisfaction. Many vets
wouldn't have bothered with the intricate piece of surgery, knowing full well that a good outcome was
unlikely.

'He's better,' Eve said delightedly. 'He's good as
new.' She came forward and wrapped her arms around
Kirsty. 'Oh, Dr Maine. Thank you.' Then, with a war-
whoop, she headed for the door. 'Mum! Kirsty's fixed
Custard. He's all better. . .' Suddenly she paused.
'You do still want me to work for you today?' she
demanded.

'I sure do,' Kirsty informed her. 'You've a debt to

pay, young lady. And your job starts right now. You, the veterinarian assistant, are required to ensure that I, the veterinarian, have another hour's uninterrupted sleep. Or you're fired, Eve Watts.'

'Yes, ma'am,' Eve said happily. 'Oh, yes. . .' And then the voice raised again in a whoop that told Kirsty any thoughts of future sleep might as well be abandoned now. 'Mum. . .'

Reid collected Kirsty half an hour after he said he would. Kirsty was waiting in Anthea's big front room. She had come home from morning surgery, showered and dressed simply in linen trousers and a light silk blouse. She looked great, Anthea had told her, but she didn't feel great.

Last night had been a crazy aberration—an episode that mustn't ever be repeated. Today she had to make that clear to Reid.

She had herself firmly in control at twelve-thirty. By the time Reid finally arrived a little after one, her self-control was slipping.

It slipped even further when she saw him walk up towards the front door. His face was lined with weariness. Kirsty's fingers itched to smooth the lines away. She crushed her hands angrily into her pockets and went to answer the door.

'Sorry I'm late.' He smiled tiredly down at her. 'I had a death.'

'Oh, Reid. . .' The concern in her voice was uncontrollable. She bit her lip. He mustn't be able to hear the love. . .

He shrugged, unconsciously taking her hand, as though he didn't know the sensation such an action caused within her. 'Old Mrs Carter. It wasn't indigestion last night.' He shrugged. 'Not a tragedy, but it was a bit close to last weekend for me to be professionally detached.'

'Are you ever professionally detached?' Kirsty asked softly, and Reid shrugged again.

'I try.'

No, Kirsty thought. No, you don't. . . Aloud, she said, 'And Ben Harsham?'

'He'll be fine.' Another weary smile. 'I've been on to the Children's Hospital. His paralysis was wearing off before he reached them. They're running a few tests today, but he should be home by road ambulance tomorrow.'

Margaret Haslett was waiting, with a warm welcoming smile and the smell of baking wafting through the farm-house. She brushed aside Kirsty's apologies for lateness as unimportant.

'I have a doctor for a son,' she said simply. 'I've learned that the clock is a very vague approximation at the best of times.'

Reid stayed silent during most of the meal but Margaret chatted happily to Kirsty, telling her Woongarra gossip and gently probing Kirsty's past. It wasn't malicious, Kirsty thought. It was wanting to know because she was genuinely interested. Kirsty didn't mind. In fact, she liked it. It was as if she was finally linking her two lives—her life before Woongarra and now. . .

As she was questioned, Kirsty spoke of her child-hood on a farm, and how hard she'd found the shift to the city for training. She spoke of the friends she'd made at university, and the likes and dislikes of each branch of the profession she had been training for.

Margaret listened and questioned. Reid just listened.

And then came the question Kirsty had known was inevitable. Margaret poured coffee for them all, sat down again, and looked at Kirsty's face. She could see that Kirsty knew she intended asking it. In a way the question had to be asked—and had to be answered.

'How long ago did your husband die, Kirsty?'

Kirsty stared down at her creamy mug of coffee. Beside her she was aware that Reid had started, and then gone completely still.

'Two years ago,' she said softly, so softly that she wasn't quite sure that she'd made herself say it.

'And how long were you married?'

'Four. . . Four years. We married early in my—in our vet course.'

'He was a vet too?'

Kirsty shook her head. The pain was etched deep behind her eyes. 'He never. . . He never qualified. He wanted to so badly. . .I went back after he died and finished, but Neil never made it.'

'I lost my husband twenty years ago,' Margaret Haslett told her, her voice gentling. 'And I miss him every day. Is it like that for you, Kirsty?'

Kirsty lifted her face. Bright unshed tears welled behind her eyes. 'I guess so,' she whispered. 'I guess so.'

They finished their coffee in silence, each deep in their own thoughts. It was strange, Kirsty thought. The silence wasn't uncomfortable. It was as if. . .as if they were a family. Each a part of the whole. Each interacting without speaking. . .

It was Reid who finally broke the stillness. He stood up and started to clear the dishes. 'I'm taking Kirsty down the back paddock to show her the waterfall,' he told his mother. 'We'll be back in about an hour. OK?'

'It's OK with me.' Margaret smiled. 'I could do with a nap. Leave those dishes, Reid. They'll be my exercise for the afternoon.' She smiled again. 'And that's all I'm doing. Yesterday I carted fifty bales of hay over to the new windbreak to act as mulch. Washing dishes is all I'm doing now for at least a week. Are you taking Misty and Miles?'

Misty and Miles. . . They must be the dogs, thought Kirsty. There was a Border Collie asleep under the table and a fat old Labrador on the front veranda.

'Of course,' Reid told her.

'Does Kirsty——?'

'Of course Kirsty does.'

But Kirsty didn't. She and Reid walked down past

the sheds behind the house with the dogs following
contentedly behind and she stopped short. Placidly
grazing in the house-paddock were two horses.

'Hi, Misty,' Reid called. 'Come on, Miles. . .'

'Miles and Misty. . .' Kirsty stopped dead. 'They're
horses.'

'Well, I guess they are,' Reid teased gently. 'They're
a bit big for dogs—or even ponies.'

Both horses were coming eagerly towards them. The
mare and gelding looked like brother and sister. They
were magnificent chestnuts, their coats glossy and their
eyes bright and eager. They trotted across the paddock,
manes flying and heads tossing in excitement. Here,
then, was action.

'Reid, I can't. . .' It was a breathless whisper of
protest, and Reid didn't hear it. He was reaching out
to take the gelding's halter in his hand, his free hand
reaching up to pat the sleek head.

'Oh, yes, there's a gallop in store for you, sir. And
one for Misty too. . .'

Misty. . . Kirsty looked up at the mare anxiously
nosing her brother aside. She was beautiful. She was
raring to go. . .

'Reid, I can't. . .'

This time he heard her. Reid turned and looked at
her white face and he left the horse he was holding.

'You can ride,' he said flatly.

'Yes. . . But. . .'

'But you don't. Because you once had a husband.'

He was so damned acute. He saw right into her.
Kirsty's heart swelled in misery. 'I promised. . .' she
whispered.

'You promised never to ride a horse again?' he
demanded.

'N-no.'

'Well, then.' He wasn't interested. Someone—it
must have been Margaret—had hung saddles,
blankets, all the tack for two horses, over the paddock
gate in readiness. Reid picked up a rug and tossed it

to Kirsty. 'Misty hasn't been ridden for two weeks. She's my mother's horse, but Mum's arthritis has been playing up. So she's a deprived horse. Either you get yourself on the horse, Dr Maine, or I report you to the Royal Society for Prevention of Cruelty to Animals.'

'Reid. . .'

'No buts, Dr Maine. Saddle your horse.'

'I don't want to.'

Reid put his saddle down on the grass. He came towards her and took her hands in his.

'Kirsty, you are aching to ride that horse. Am I wrong or am I right?'

'No. Yes. . .' She pulled away, anger and despair welling within. 'Yes. I want to ride her. But I promised Neil. . .'

'You promised him you'd never ride again?' Reid's voice was incredulous, and Kirsty shook her head.

'What did you promise him, then, Kirsty?'

Kirsty looked up helplessly at Reid. It would be so easy. . . To tell him and let him sweep her doubts aside. Easy but dishonest.

'No.'

He looked at her in baffled anger. Clearly this was not what Reid Haslett was used to in conducting his courtships. A woman who held a barrier before her—a barrier of pain.

'If you didn't promise you'd never ride a horse again, then saddle Misty and get up,' he said roughly, as though weary of the argument. 'I'm taking you down the bottom paddock to show you the waterfall, and the only way to get there is by horse. So you saddle your horse or I throw you up before me. And it's a fair distance. Miles will be sweating by the end of it if he has to carry both of us. If you want to do that to a horse, Kirsty Maine. . .'

'That's not fair.'

'That's the way it is, Kirsty.' His voice was implacable. 'Get yourself on a horse or be put.'

Kirsty looked up at him and his eyes held nothing

but determination. Nothing? Maybe there was also a
trace of humour there too.

'Damn you. . .' she said desperately.

'Saddle your horse, Kirsty,' he said kindly. 'And you
don't have to damn me. I already am.'

Kirsty stood and stared indecisively as Reid threw
the rug over his horse, following it with a worn, well-
polished saddle. To get on a horse again. . .

Reid's words had been implacable. Ride or be forc-
ibly made to ride. Do it with dignity or without. . .

He meant it, Kirsty knew. He was trying to push
her through the barrier of pain he sensed she had. He
knew her. . . I must be more like Stephanie than just
in appearance, she thought bitterly, for him to know
me so well. . .

She turned back to Misty. The mare nudged her
face, her nostrils steaming hopefully against Kirsty's
cheek. Kirsty pushed her away with a shaky laugh.

'There's no need to kiss me. I haven't taken you for
a ride yet.'

She picked up the rug Reid had thrown her and
which she'd let slide to the ground. It seemed it was
time to ride. Time to ride again. . .

Reid didn't speak. He finished saddling Miles,
mounted, and then stayed watching Kirsty as she tightened the girth and checked her stirrup leathers for
length. His eyes were frankly appraising. He knew this
had once been second nature to her. . .

Kirsty lifted herself lightly on to the saddle and Reid
grinned.

'You've done that a thousand times in your life,
Kirsty Maine.'

Kirsty didn't answer. She couldn't. Memories were
all around her—memories and a sense of betrayal.

'Come on, then,' Reid told her. 'We've a mile of
open ground before it gets too wooded to gallop. And
I'll bet that's just what these beauties want to do, isn't
it, Miles?'

He left her to follow. Misty took a couple of eager

paces forward, but Kirsty held her lightly back. Not yet.

Reid didn't stop. He looked back once and then seemed to sense that she would follow. Eventually. He knew instinctively that Kirsty needed to do this alone.

He cantered on, a man at one with his horse. His hands were light on his horse's mouth; there was no need to pull and jab at Miles to have him follow Reid's will. Man and horse had ridden so often together they were a team. One. . .

Dear God, Kirsty thought bleakly. She couldn't be jealous of a horse. She couldn't. . .

Kirsty's hands lifted, her heels touched the mare's quiveringly eager flanks, and she started down the long stretch of open country before the distant hills. She began to follow.

It was as good as it had ever been. This was a part of her that Kirsty had locked away. Reid had said she had done this a thousand times. More. Since her father had tossed her up on a horse before she could walk, she had ridden. A horse had been her life. With Neil trotting proudly beside her on his very own pony as she learned—Neil scorning her because she was afraid of trying a jump—Neil laughing with triumph as she'd tried and failed, and then tried and won. . .

Neil had been there forever. They had been raised almost as brother and sister, and marriage had just been an extension of a partnership which had no beginning. It had always been there.

Neil. . . Home. . . Her horses. . . She could hardly remember one without the other.

And now there was a horse under her and a man flying ahead who wasn't Neil, and her heart was crying out to follow.

A ride, she promised herself. A ride is all this is. One good gallop on a lovely mare. Hardly a betrayal, Kirsty Maine.

The mare's stride lengthened imperceptibly. Kirsty didn't check her. The mare felt the difference—or

was it indifference? It couldn't be. Misty flattened her
ears and headed for her brother. Down, down the
long, green paddock, the wind flying through Kirsty's
hair, and the salt tears stinging her cheeks as remembrance mingled with relief. Neil wouldn't have wanted
her to lose this. He wouldn't. . .

And then Reid was reining in, turning to wait for
her and falling in effortlessly beside her, Miles's strides
shortening to match those of the mare. They were
together, and the hills were before them.

Last night was nothing to this, Kirsty thought. This
wasn't like making love to a man. This was. . .

And then she glanced sideways at the man beside
her and she knew that this was just an extension of
last night. They might as well have been making love.
They weren't touching, but the pounding hooves, the
wind on her damp face and the warmth of the strength
between her legs. . . Reid was here. Reid was with
her. He looked across at her and his black eyes laughed
at her—loved her—and Kirsty was spinning wildly in
a vortex of emotion she had never felt in her life.

And then the hills were before them and they had
to check, slowing as the ground underneath became
rough and treacherous.

Reid led the way through the trees, following a rough
path where the only mode of transport would be horses
or walking. The eucalypts here were massive for coastal
timber, blocking out the sun and making the path cool
and inviting. The horses walked slowly, drinking in the
coolness and the familiar scents.

'Nearly there,' Reid said softly, but Kirsty had
already heard the first faint sounds of water pounding
over rocks. The horses heard too, or maybe they
already knew what was in store. Their walk quickened
and two minutes later they burst out into the clearing
around the waterfall.

It was a magic place. The rock wall climbed high
into the hills, and clear, cold water cascaded down into
a deep pool of sapphire-green. The pool was deep and

translucent. Bright fish flashed silver in the depths and a crane was preening itself on the bank. The bird must have known the horses. It didn't stop its ablutions for a moment.

Misty put her head down to follow her brother's example, plunging her nose into the delicious mountain water. Kirsty let her have her way, sliding off her back and staring appreciatively around her.

'It. . . It's beautiful,' she said.

'It is,' Reid answered, but he wasn't looking at the water. He was looking straight at Kirsty.

Kirsty took a deep breath. 'Thank you. . .thank you for showing it to me.' Her tone was absurdly formal. She waited breathlessly until the mare's head came up. 'Do we. . .? I mean. . .can we go back now? We told your mother an hour. . .'

'We've been gone only half that.'

'But what if you're called?' Kirsty was aware that she sounded like a frightened child, and Reid smiled as he crossed to where she stood. He lifted a beeper from his pocket.

'Then I'm called. But for now. . .'

'Reid, no!'

It was a frightened wail, but it didn't stop Reid.

'For now, my Kirsty, we go for a swim. You can't come to a place like this on a day like today and not swim. The gods of the place would be offended.'

'Then they'll just have to be offended,' Kirsty said with asperity. 'Reid, I didn't bring my bathers.'

'Silly me.' Reid's smile deepened. 'I can fix that.' And before Kirsty knew what he was about, he had her in his arms. He lifted her high and strode strongly to the water's edge, where the rocks dropped sharply away to the sparkling depths.

'Put me down. Reid Haslett, put me down. . .' It was a frightened wail.

'Yes, ma'am.'

And he swung her up and tossed her easily as far out into the pool as he could throw.

Kirsty sank like a stone.

It was a conscious decision to sink. The ice-coldness of the water shocked her into breathlessness, but Kirsty had swum like a fish since babyhood. Instinctively she would have knifed upward through the water—up into the dappled sunlight—up to Reid. . .

Instead, she let her body go down, down, to where the wisping fronds of underwater reeds touched her face as she lay deliberately among them.

She could stay down here for minutes. She knew she could. It had been a favourite pastime of Kirsty and Neil as children, and Reid Haslett deserved a good fright. To throw her in when he didn't even know if she could swim. . . Well, she wasn't the only one who'd get wet!

She started counting in her head, a method of extending the breath in her lungs, and forced her body into limp and lifeless stillness.

The water cascading down the falls was moving the pool, and her seemingly lifeless body swayed with the motion. It was beautiful down here. Thirty-three. . . Thirty-four. . .

And then a force was diving like an arrow through the water. Hands were gripping her, hauling her, and just for a moment Kirsty dug her toes into the soft mud at the base of the lagoon, giving the impression that she was caught. It was for a millisecond only, but she felt the dragging increase in urgency. She was giving Reid Haslett the fright of his life, and he deserved it.

Did he? Her body lay limply in his arms as he hauled her to the surface. Her actions had been a spur of the moment anger at his thoughtlessness, but now. . .

He was as skilled in the water as she was, his strength pushing her body up, up towards the light. Her face broke through the surface, she took a lovely gasp of the warm air and then dived down again.

Reid couldn't believe it. She watched him from below as he trod water, his fully clothed body hanging still in the water. Even his boots, she thought with satisfaction. She had been wearing casual sneakers which would dry easily. His boots were leather and would take days. . .

She turned towards the cascade of water, her arms pulling her through the water like a fish. When she resurfaced it was under the crystal-cold rain. She hauled herself on to a rock, sat with the water splashing down over her face, and watched with interest.

Anger? she wondered.

He had turned in the water to watch where she had gone. Now he trod water for a moment, before finally making up his mind. He swam strongly over to her and surfaced by her rock.

'If I were you I'd take your boots off,' Kirsty said kindly. 'They're heavier than mine. They'll weigh you down.'

'My God, Kirsty. . .' He reached out to grab her ankle but she was too quick for him, sliding back further behind the wall of water. 'Did Neil ever horsewhip you?' Reid demanded.

The laughter-lines around Kirsty's eyes disappeared with a snap. Neil. . .

Enough. Enough.

She stood, edging herself along the ledge behind the waterfall until she reached dry ground. For a moment she had almost forgotten.

Misty was idly nibbling the grass at the water's edge. As Kirsty approached her the mare edged away, unwilling to be parted from this lush feed. Before Kirsty could reach her, Reid had come up behind and swung her round to face him.

'Coward,' he said softly.

Kirsty gasped. 'How dare you. . .?'

'You're hiding behind Neil's memory, aren't you?'

'Don't be stupid.'

'You can't hold Neil between you and the world forever,' he said softly. 'Especially when you feel like this. . .'

'Reid, don't. . .' It was a frantic wail. Reid had put his arms around her, pulling her body back to his. Her back moulded to his body. . . The wetness of their clothes made them almost disappear. She could feel his strength, his warmth and his desire.

There was no doubting that he wanted her. And she wanted him so much. . .

'No!' Somehow she found the strength to pull away and turn to face him. 'No.'

'That's not what you said last night.'

'And last night I was a little crazy. A lot crazy! I'm not crazy any more.' She took a deep breath. 'Reid, my husband died two years ago and I promised him that no one—*no one*—would ever take his place. I don't intend to break that promise, Reid Haslett. So leave me alone.'

'You promised——'

'I don't want to talk about it, Reid. Not now. Not ever.' She walked over and caught Misty's rein. Swiftly she mounted, and sat looking down at Reid's shadowed face.

'Not ever,' she whispered.

And she turned Misty's head for home.

Reid followed Kirsty slowly home. By the time he arrived, Kirsty had removed Misty's saddle and was rubbing her down. She ignored Reid as he rode towards her. For the life of her she couldn't think what else to do.

Reid sat looking at her for a long moment but she kept right on brushing. Brushing as if her life depended on it.

'You'll take the oil out of her coat if you keep brushing so hard.'

'It won't hurt. It's warm enough.'

'Kirsty. . .'

'Just shut up and let me get on with it.' Kirsty was crying and she couldn't have turned towards him to save herself. She wouldn't let him see just how much pain she was in.

'Leave it, Kirsty.' He swung down from his saddle and his hand came down over hers, stilling the brush. 'I'll do it later.'

'I won't have any man doing my work for me. I won't have anyone.' Kirsty gulped unromantically and fought for possession of her hand. 'I'm on my own, Reid Haslett. I promised Neil. . .' She took a deep breath. 'Please don't make me break that promise.'

'I'm not Neil, Kirsty. You loved Neil and Neil has died. That doesn't mean your love for him has died, or that by loving me you'll forget Neil. Our love is new and different. I can't replace Neil and I don't want to.'

'But you're replacing Stephanie. . .'

She hadn't meant to say it. It just fell out.

It was true, though. It had to be. Would anyone believe it was crazy coincidence that Reid Haslett had fallen in love with his ex-wife's double? Crazy, crazy, crazy. . .

Reid's hand still held hers. Slowly he turned her around to face him and she was powerless against the strength of those hands.

'Kirsty Maine, I am not replacing my ex-wife. I never would. I made a giant mistake marrying Stephanie, and until I met you I thought that mistake would scar me forever. I've met a new woman, though—a woman I can trust and love with all my heart. A new and wondrous love.' He lifted her chin so that he could look down at her tear-strewn cheeks. 'Kirsty, I'm asking for that love to be returned. I want a new life, and I want it for us together. Would Neil forbid that?'

'Neil wouldn't—— It would be different if Neil had forbidden. . .but I promised.'

'And you won't break that promise.'

Kirsty looked up at him, her heart wrenching within her.

'I can't,' she whispered bleakly. 'I can't. Please, Reid. . . Please just leave me alone.'

'No.' He shook his head. He glanced up at his watch.

'Mum will have a cup of tea waiting at the house, Kirsty. Go up and keep her company while I fix the horses.'

'But——'

'Go for now, Kirsty,' he said gently. He touched her face fleetingly with his finger. 'For now you need a little space, but that's all I'm giving you. I'm not leaving you alone, Kirsty. Not now. Not ever.'

Somehow Kirsty made it up to the house. Margaret still seemed to be sleeping. Kirsty put the big black kettle into the middle of the range and found what she needed to make tea. As the kettle started to hiss over the fire Margaret came into the room.

'You're back,' she smiled. 'How was my Misty?'

'Beautiful,' Kirsty said unsteadily. 'Just beautiful.'

'She is, isn't she?' Margaret's voice had changed. She came across to where Kirsty was intent on pouring scoops of tea into the china teapot. One for each person and one for the pot. . . Hard to concentrate all her energies into such a simple task.

'What's wrong, Kirsty?'

'Nothing.' Kirsty's voice was a whisper, and a stupid tear fell down and splashed among the tealeaves.

Margaret frowned. 'You're wet.'

'I am.' Kirsty took a deep breath, fighting for control. 'Your son threw me in the lagoon.'

'Reid. . .' And then Margaret stared as her son came in through the door. Reid's heavier clothes were more sodden than Kirsty's. She looked back to Kirsty, dawning respect in her eyes.

'And you threw him in too, I suppose?'

'Your future daughter-in-law has a wicked, conniving mind.' Reid grinned. 'She's not to be trusted.'

'Future——'

'No!' Kirsty turned towards Reid and backed to the door. 'Don't do this to me, Reid. Don't. . .I won't. . . Margaret, I'm sorry, but Reid has rocks in his head. I'm not your future daughter-in-law.'

'Reid, what are you doing?' Margaret said worriedly. 'Just because Kirsty's so like Stephanie. . .'

'There,' Kirsty whispered. 'Even your mother. . .'

'It's not anything to do with Stephanie.' Reid crossed to Kirsty. 'For heaven's sake, Kirsty. . .'

Kirsty ignored him. Her car. . . Her kingdom for a car. Why had she allowed Reid to drive her here? Desperately she turned to Margaret. 'Reid brought me here.' She took a deep breath. 'But, please. . . Margaret, you drive?'

'Yes.'

'Will you take me home, then, please?'

Margaret looked from Reid to Kirsty and back again.

'Of course I will, Kirsty,' she said gently.

'Don't be a fool,' Reid said, and his mother turned on him.

'There's only one fool in this room, Reid Haslett,' his mother said soundly. 'And it's not Kirsty and it's not me. Now, I suggest you go and take a shower and get into some clean clothes. You're making puddles on my kitchen floor.'

'I'll drive Kirsty home.'

'No.' Kirsty held up a hand in futile denial, but it was enough to stop Reid as he crossed the room towards her. 'Reid. . . Reid, I'm not your wife.' She took a deep breath. 'From the moment we met you've thought I was someone else. Well, I'm the local vet, Reid. That's all. Your mother's friend and the local vet. And, please. . . That's the only relationship I want with you.'

CHAPTER TEN

WHAT followed was the loneliest week Kirsty had ever known. Even the week Neil died hadn't seemed so bleak. Neil's death had been expected. It had been a release, and mixed with her grief had been a relief that Neil was free of pain. Released. . .

Now. . . The pain was almost as raw, and there was no mitigating sense of relief. Only a dull, aching void that she knew could never be filled.

Her work was her only release. She moved from farm to farm and back to the surgery, putting everything she had into the treatment of her patients. Anthea, now settled happily in as full-time receptionist, watched her with troubled eyes but said nothing. Anthea had known enough pain to sense when others were feeling it, but she was also sensitive enough to desist from probing.

Reid hadn't come near her.

'He won't,' Margaret Haslett had promised when she dropped Kirsty off at Anthea's on Saturday afternoon. 'I'll tell him you asked me to relay a message to stay clear. He needs time to cool down. Kirsty, I don't know what's driving him. He was so darned hurt by Stephanie. I can't believe he's acting this way with you. He must. . .I guess he must still love her.'

It was the logical thing to believe, Kirsty thought bitterly—Reid betrayed by his wife, and then finding her double. Reid wanting to take another chance.

'Know that you are loved.' Kirsty whispered Reid's words to herself over and over again as she went about her duties. Who was loved, though? Stephanie? Kirsty? Or a crazy, impossible mixture?

Her promise to Neil hung around her, but it no longer seemed a tie. It seemed a defence against

156

stupidity. A defence against letting her body betray her as it so easily had.

She hadn't seen Reid for a week now, and she wouldn't. Not unless there was an emergency that required them both—and surely by then she would have her emotions under some sort of control.

'I'm off to the Hendersons',' she told Anthea as she bade her last patients—a basket of wriggling pups brought in for vaccination—farewell. 'The mare I treated is due to have her stitches removed.'

'She's OK?' Anthea looked up from her filing.

'She's fine. The Hendersons have been lucky.' Kirsty frowned. 'They're going to have to do something about stables pretty soon, though. The mares are going to start foaling within the next couple of weeks.'

'There's plenty of good stabling at my place,' Anthea said off-handedly. 'I don't suppose. . .'

Kirsty stopped and stared. 'Of course.' She frowned. 'Have you mentioned it to Bob?'

'No. It's not. . . It's not a professional stable or anything.'

'Not now, but it was, and it could be again without too much trouble. You trained horses.' Kirsty thought. 'There's plenty of feed in the paddocks. Bob would have to bring the mares over soon, though, as they'll be too close to their time. But it's only a couple of miles. The ones we're worried about could be walked slowly.'

'Look, Kirsty. . .' Anthea shifted uneasily in her chair. 'Look, I don't want——'

'You don't want what?'

'If I ask Bob, he'll think I'm just trying to make some money. . .'

'Which you are.' Kirsty grinned down at her. 'For heaven's sake, Anthea Watts, you're a businesswoman without a business. Bob Henderson has a huge insurance pay-out and nowhere to put his horses for three or four months until the stables are rebuilt. You have twenty or more stables and a bank mortgage that's screaming for help. So put the two of them together.'

'I couldn't. . .'

'But I could.' Kirsty smiled. 'It would make a difference to your nice, quiet lifestyle, though. All those pregnant mares. . . And you'd have to accommodate some of the lads. It's pretty intensive for the few weeks after foaling.'

'There's rooms over the stables.' Anthea was scarcely breathing. 'I could clean them out.'

'We could clean them out over the weekend,' Kirsty told her. 'Or we'll hire a cleaning lady.'

'Hire. . .' Anthea took a deep breath. 'What with, for heaven's sake?'

'With your new-found wealth.' Kirsty grinned. 'Now, shall I ask Mr Henderson if he's interested?'

'Kirsty Maine. . .' Anthea had risen, but she sat down now with an audible plonk. 'Kirsty Maine, you just go ahead and ask him.'

The mare's leg had healed beautifully. Bob Henderson himself held her head as Kirsty carefully removed the dressing and the thread. For the last few days the dressing hadn't been necessary for anything but to prevent the mare biting at the stitches. She hadn't touched them, though.

Kirsty stood back in satisfaction, eased herself out of kicking range, and motioned for Bob to let her go.

'All fixed,' she said happily. 'Now all she has to do is concentrate on her pregnancy.'

'She'll be one of the early ones, I reckon,' Bob told her. 'She's not due for two weeks but by the look of her I reckon she'll be early.' He clenched his fists. 'Now her stitches are out I think her owner will come and take her to other stables. Give High Born a miss for this season.'

'Why?' Kirsty already knew why, but she was giving Anthea her best shot.

'You know how the system works?' Bob asked, and Kirsty nodded.

A stallion might be capable of serving forty or more mares in the season. Each service was termed a nomination. After contracting for a nomination, the mare's owners stabled the mare near the stallion for the few weeks before her foal dropped. The mare came into season usually about nine days to two weeks after foaling, and shifting her so soon after foaling was risky. So a mare would foal at Bob Henderson's stable and be served by High Born before she returned to her home stable—hopefully pregnant again.

'We've tried to keep the fire quiet,' Bob told her. 'But the racing industry has its own grapevine, despite us being so far away. The last couple of days I've been getting calls from owners worried about their mares. The thought of letting the mares drop out in the paddocks is clearly upsetting them.'

'I don't blame them,' Kirsty told him. 'With the money invested in this bloodstock, I'd want them foaling where I could keep an eye on them too.'

'Yeah. . .' He sighed. 'I've been coming to the same conclusion. At this time of year I can't depend on good weather. But where does that leave me?' Bob dug his hands in his pockets. 'I'm insured against loss from the fire, but the loss of full service fees is going to be hard for the insurance company to swallow. The services aren't paid for until a positive pregnancy test—forty-two days after service.'

A service with a stallion such as High Born could well be worth thirty thousand dollars or more. Thirty multiplied by. . . Kirsty did some fast sums and winced. 'Have you thought of alternative stabling?'

'Oh, yeah. . .' Bob grimaced. 'But putting horses all over the place is hardly satisfactory. And High Born has to be close. . .'

'How about the stabling at Anthea Watts' farm?'

They had been walking back to the house. Now Bob Henderson stopped dead in his tracks. 'The Watts place. . .?'

'There's more than twenty usable stables. There are

a couple of separate ones where High Born could be placed. The stables are well-built, and there are rooms above for men you'd like to stay there.'

'You're kidding.' He frowned. 'I haven't been near the place since——'

'Since Anthea's husband did a bunk.' Kirsty grimaced. 'Not many people have. Anthea's kept to herself. But it's still a workable stable.'

'But she'll have horses. . .'

Kirsty understood that. No stud-owner would introduce his horses to a bunch of riding-school hacks whose immune status could be suspect.

'One child's pony. Nine years old and I'll vouch for its health.'

Bob whistled, his mind obviously racing from angle to angle. 'Do you reckon she'd come at the invasion?' he asked slowly. 'It'd mean the place would be overrun with my horses and my men. And it'd be run on my terms.'

'Anthea's having trouble meeting her mortgage,' Kirsty said honestly. 'Her husband left her in a mess. If you presented her with a good enough financial proposition she might be talked into it.' She smiled inwardly as she said it. She'd have to get back to Anthea fast to stop her jumping at first offer.

'Fair enough.' The farmer grinned across at Kirsty, as though guessing her thoughts. 'Fair enough.'

A man came from around the back of the house, leading a horse, and Kirsty stopped as she recognised High Born. High Born stopped as well, staring belligerently at Kirsty and Bob—his owner. What conspiracy is this? the horse's stance seemed to be saying, and Kirsty smiled.

'No problems?' she asked Bob, and Bob shook his head.

'He's OK.' He motioned to the man leading the big horse. 'He's even behaving for Dougal. Fred—my head lad—is out of action during foaling because of his arm. I'm lost without him, so I contacted Dougal on the off-chance that he was free. Dougal left here three years ago to try his luck in the city. Didn't like it much, it seems, 'cause he jumped at the chance to come back. Even when Fred's back I can use someone of Dougal's calibre. Dougal Blainey, meet Dr Maine.'

Dougal, a wiry, soft-spoken man in his thirties, smiled shyly. 'Bob didn't have to ask very often,' he confessed. 'After three years in Melbourne the wife and I have decided this is a better place to bring up kids.' He looked over to where a small boy was perched on a rail, watching proceedings. 'Damned unhealthy place, the city. Mark has asthma. He's going on for three and he just isn't doing any good.'

As if to prove his point, the child started to cough. He jumped down from the rail, a frail, undersized waif of a child, looked uncertainly at the group around his father, and made his way back towards the house. Kirsty stared after him, her heart almost stopping.

Asthma. . .

'Is that Mark's usual cough?' she asked.

'Yeah.' The man grimaced. 'He's got so much bloody muck in his chest. I reckon if we could only get rid of it. . .'

'And the doctor says it's asthma?'

'We've got the pumps and everything. Fat lot of good they do, though. The last doctor we went to said we should take him into the Children's Hospital for assessment, but we. . . Well, we decided to come home. Give the kid a chance.'

'Poor little blighter,' Bob said easily. 'He'll do all right here, though, Dougal. Look at me. An asthmatic at sixty and it hasn't killed me yet.'

'Dougal. . .' Kirsty fought for words. Her mind was almost numbly still. That cough. . . She had grown up with that cough. 'Dougal, how long is it since you saw a doctor?' she asked.

He was surprised. 'I dunno. A month. Maybe less. The wife had him there just before we left Melbourne, I think.'

'Dougal, Mark's cough doesn't sound asthmatic. It's full of phlegm. I reckon. . .I reckon you should take him back in and see what Dr Haslett says.'

'You reckon there might be an infection?' The man stared at her. 'But he always sounds like that.'

'Couldn't hurt to take him in though, Dougal,' Bob told him. 'Doc Haslett's OK. And, if the kid is asthmatic, it doesn't hurt to let the doctor get to know him before he has a bad attack.' He grimaced. 'I ought to know. I remember as a kid being in a full-blown attack and being thrown into the care of strange doctors. Didn't help.'

The man nodded. 'Yeah.' He turned to Kirsty. 'Thanks for your interest.' He smiled. 'We'll take him in in the morning. It'd be a laugh if we moved all the way back here to help his asthma and it just turned out to be a long-term infection, wouldn't it?'

Laugh. . . It was the last thing Kirsty felt like doing. If her suspicions were right. . .

She felt sick. The little boy was peering round the corner of the buildings, waiting for his father to be finished with these strangers. Kirsty looked over at the little white face and felt like bursting into tears.

She was going to have to talk to Reid. The thought made her feel even worse, but she had set it up now so that Dougal and his wife would bring the little boy in to see Reid the next morning. Reid had to know her suspicions.

So telephone. . .

That would be worse, she thought. But Reid did his hospital rounds about now. If she caught him in the hospital corridor then she could voice her suspicions with other people around. Walk up to the sister's station, ask for Reid, tell him what she wanted to tell him and then leave. . .

She would see him again. . .

It's not that at all, she told herself crossly but she knew it was. It had been over a week. . .

'Drat the man!'

She spoke aloud as she returned to the car, and one of the stable-lads looked up in astonishment.

Oh, great, she thought grimly. Now he'll tell his boss the new vet's unstable. That's all I need. . .

She had been right when she guessed where Reid would be. The sister looked up and smiled as Kirsty made her request. 'He's in with Tom Harsham,' she told her. 'He should be finished in a moment. If you'd like to take a seat. . .'

Tom Harsham. . . Kirsty frowned. 'What's Tom in for?'

'Pneumonia,' the girl told her, and Kirsty nodded. Tom had coughed and coughed. It made sense.

'I'll bet he had to be dragged in with a bulldozer.' She smiled and the girl smiled back.

'When his wife brought their little boy back from Melbourne she took one look and drove him in. Believe it or not, he's so sick he's grateful to be here, but it's nearly choking him that he needs us.'

And then Reid was coming down the corridor towards them. Kirsty looked up and her face drained of colour.

He wasn't supposed to look like this. He wasn't. . . She loved him so much it was as though there was a physical void in her soul. Only he could fill it.

'Kirsty——' He caught himself. 'Dr Maine. How may I help you?'

His tone was formal, but his eyes were caressing. Kirsty's heart was doing back-flips.

Formal. . . She had to be formal too.

'Reid. . . Dr Haslett, I saw a child today. . .' Her voice drained away, and she knew her colour was going with it. The thought of what lay ahead. . .

He was with her then, his hand under her elbow, gently guiding her, out of sight of the sister's station and into his inner office.

'What is it, Kirsty?' he asked gently, and his voice made Kirsty blink. 'What's wrong?'

'There's nothing wrong with me,' she made herself say. 'But there's a new stable-lad working for Bob Henderson. Dougal Blainey. . .'

'I know him. He's a local who's been away.'

'He has a son. A little boy. . .' Kirsty's voice trailed off miserably.

'And?' Reid had crossed to the other side of the desk, putting distance between himself and Kirsty. It was as if he needed it. Now he looked at her white drawn face and the effort to keep himself on that side of the desk was enormous. 'You're rushing the girl like a bull at a gate,' his mother had told him. 'For heaven's sake, don't you see the child has her own shadows?'

There was a shadow there now. It was all over her face, making her writhe in misery, and only his mother's unequivocable words stopped him taking her into his arms.

'And. . .' Kirsty took a deep breath. 'He's frail and tiny for a three-year-old. He coughs and coughs. His father tells me it's asthma, and that's one of the reasons they moved back to the country.' She raised fearful eyes to Reid. 'But, Reid, I don't think it is. The cough. . . It's not dry. It's full of phlegm, and his father says he coughs like that all the time. . .'

'And you think. . .?'

'I think he has cystic fibrosis.'

There. The thing was said. The words were out, like a death-sentence, hanging in the air between them.

Reid's expression stilled. His face was watchful. 'Why do you think that?'

Kirsty raised miserable eyes to Reid's face. 'I know that cough,' she whispered. 'I lived with it.'

'Neil?'

He knew. He could see. . .

Kirsty nodded. Then Reid was walking around the desk, taking her shoulders in his hands and pressing her into the chair. 'Tell me about it, Kirsty.'

'There's no need.'

'I think there is.'

She raised fearful eyes to his, but his face was calm, compassionate but detached. He was making no demands except for information. And maybe. . . Maybe he had the right to know. But it was so hard. . .

'Neil was the son of our neighbours——' Kirsty started. She turned towards the window. Down below the hospital the lights of the harbour were just flickering on in the gathering dusk. 'They had problems. Neil's father was an alcoholic and his mother struggled to keep the family together. Neil was their youngest and, when he was four, he was diagnosed as having cystic fibrosis. The outlook at that time was so limited. They told his parents that he'd be lucky to make it to twenty. And his parents. . .' Kirsty took a deep breath. 'His parents had four other healthy children, and his father said if he was going to die they weren't going to let the whole family suffer. So they decided to put him in foster-care.'

Reid winced. He said nothing, though. He kept looking at Kirsty and Kirsty kept looking down at the harbour.

'My parents were appalled,' she said. 'Neil was two years older than me. They'd had me after three miscarriages and they'd been told they couldn't have any more children. Neil. . . Well, Neil was always in and out of our place. My mother had clucked over him since he could walk across the road, and he and my father were mates. So they brought Neil home.'

'A courageous decision.'

Kirsty shook her head. 'I used to think so,' she whispered. 'But Mum told me that it would have been much harder to live with themselves if they had known Neil was being placed in one foster-home after another. He was such. . . He was such a gentle person. He didn't deserve what life dished up to him.'

'So you were brought up together.'

'He was my big brother,' Kirsty whispered. 'My friend. I loved him. . .'

'And you married him.'

Kirsty shrugged. 'Marriage was an extension of what we had. Neil had always felt. . . He'd always felt as though he was somehow beholden. Not really part of us. As he became more and more unwell that feeling intensified. By marrying. . . Well, by my marrying Neil, he was ours forever. He belonged. He had a rightful place in our lives that was legal as well as emotional and that was. . .that was so important to Neil. So important to all of us.'

'And you had four years.'

Kirsty lifted her chin. She shook her head. 'I had Neil all my life,' she said proudly. 'And I still have him. He's part of me.'

'I can see that,' Reid said gently. He hesitated. 'The funding for your surgery? If your parents didn't fund it, and it didn't come from a divorce settlement. . . Surely if Neil had cystic fibrosis he wouldn't have been able to insure his life?'

It was none of his business, Kirsty thought fleetingly, and yet, in a sense, it was. He had to know.

'Neil's parents' farm,' Kirsty told him. 'Apparently it was in Neil's mother's name. Neil's family stayed there all the time Neil was growing up but they wouldn't have anything to do with Neil. Every now and then Neil's mother would come over—when the rest of them were away—but that was the only contact Neil ever had. The kids drifted off one after the other, his father died of liver failure, and his mother soon after. She left the farm to Neil.'

'That must have caused some repercussions.'

'It did.' Kirsty smiled ruefully. 'The other children were livid but Neil was well enough to fight the challenge in the courts. When the judge found out what his parents had done to Neil he threw the objection out. And then, of course, Neil left it to me—and I was darned if I'd let his family have it. I sold it and bought the surgery.' She smiled wryly. 'Neil's gift to me. One of a million. . .'

'So you married him when he was ill?'

'He was always ill,' Kirsty said softly. 'Some times he was better than others, but he was always ill.' She took a deep breath. 'And, Reid, I think Mark Blainey has it. The symptoms point to it.'

'I can't do anything unless they bring him in to me, Kirsty.'

'That's just it. I persuaded them to come. They're bringing in Mark tomorrow. I thought——'

'You thought you'd tell me what to look for.'

Kirsty's eyes flashed up at him. 'You're. . .you're offended?'

'No.' He reached out and took her hands. 'Not offended. One professional to another. But it's not just professional, is it, Kirsty? There's not a lot of professional detachment here.'

'I can't. . . If he has what Neil had. . .'

'It might not be such a death-sentence,' Reid said bluntly. 'Twenty years has seen massive changes in the treatment of cystic fibrosis. There are many young adults leading healthy lives—and as the management of childhood fibrocystic disease improves, so the long-term damage is lessened. That means longer lives. By the time young Mark reaches adulthood, who knows? So, if I have to tell his parents that their son has cystic fibrosis, I won't necessarily be handing them a death-sentence.'

'No, but——'

'And there are other things it could be. Like you, if the coughing's moist and he's not thriving then I'll doubt the diagnosis of asthma. But it could be bronchiectasis. . .'

'Chronic infection?'

'Damage from chronic infection. If doctors treat asthma instead of infection then you get damage to the bronchial wall—secretion accumulates, eroding and further weakening the bronchus. It's a vicious circle.'

'But not. . .'

'Not fatal.' Reid smiled reassuringly. 'We have a physiotherapist visiting the hospital once a week. With care to contain further infection, and with physiotherapy to clear accumulated secretion, then Mark could live to a ripe old age.'

'But we don't know. . .'

'We don't know.' Reid cupped her chin in his hand and his eyes held hers. 'Tomorrow I'll see Mark and organise a sweat test. That'll tell me whether cystic fibrosis is on the cards. Meanwhile. . . Meanwhile there's no sense breaking your heart, Kirsty Maine. No sense at all.'

'No. . .' Stupid to think that her heart was breaking regardless.

'Kirsty. . .'

She pulled away, but the hand held her. Strong and warm. 'Kirsty, if I married you, do you really think I'd be replacing Neil?'

Kirsty's eyes widened. She said nothing and her heart grew still.

'Kirsty, Neil was part of your childhood. He was your friend, your family, your love. He's part of you. He's part of what you are, and he always will be. When you promised him that no man would ever take his place, you were right. No man ever will. Because he was Neil and you loved him. And I'm Reid Haslett, and you love me too, don't you Kirsty?'

Both hands were holding her face. His eyes were compelling, holding her to him. His eyes were making her heart make promises she couldn't. . .shouldn't keep. . .

'No. . .'

'Liar. . .'

Kirsty closed her eyes. If only she didn't look so much like Stephanie it would be easy to let this man love her—comfort her—warm her from within.

'Look at me, Kirsty.'

She wouldn't. She'd drown in his eyes.

A knock at the door saved her. Reid swore softly

and put her away from him. 'Yes?'

The sister opened the door. She looked from Reid to Kirsty and back again, and then shook her head.

'You are just so like Mrs Haslett.' She smiled at Kirsty. 'I mean the ex-Mrs Haslett. I just can't believe it.' She grinned suddenly. 'Wouldn't it be funny if you two made a match of it? You wouldn't have to pay for another set of wedding-photos.'

Reid winced. He looked swiftly down at Kirsty but her face was blank. The pain was all inward.

'I've just taken Mr Harsham's obs,' the nurse said, oblivious to the effects of her words. 'Doctor, his temp's up to forty point two.'

'Damn.' Reid frowned. 'He should be responding to the penicillin by now.'

'I'll leave you to it,' Kirsty managed. She had done what she came for. 'Let me know. . . Let me know about Mark, please, Reid.'

She pushed blindly past the nurse, out along the corridor, and into the night.

CHAPTER ELEVEN

IT WAS a long night. Somehow Kirsty managed a little sleep, but not enough. Not enough to drive away the demons making shadows around her eyes. Anthea looked up in concern as Kirsty came in for breakfast.

'You look like death,' she said bluntly. 'If I were a cow feeling poorly today I'd choose another vet. I might catch something from you.'

'Thanks a heap.' Kirsty picked up the kettle and started making herself a mug of coffee. She looked suspiciously over at Anthea. 'So what's making you so darned chipper?'

'Ten thousand dollars.'

'Ten. . .' Kirsty plonked herself down on the kitchen chair and stared. 'Run that past me again?'

'Ten thousand dollars.' Anthea chuckled and her laugh was almost girlish. 'Bob Henderson rang me last night. He's been on to his insurance company and he's covered for alternative stabling while he rebuilds. They'll cover him for twelve thousand. He figures he'll spend two thousand on extra transport if he uses my place and he's offered the rest to me for the use of my stables and my land. Ten thousand dollars! I can refurbish them for a fraction of that, so my profit margin's huge. He even reckons it might be long-term. He's tight on land, and he wouldn't mind having separate stabling accommodation during his busy periods. So now. . . So now I'm employed and I'm a landlady and I'm agisting horses. All since you came. Kirsty Maine, I could kiss you.'

And she rose and did.

Kirsty was stunned. She had had no idea of agistment charges. 'This should help with the debts,' she said weakly.

'It'll cover the worst of them.' Anthea sat down again. 'It'll mean we can start again. We can live normally. If I still have my job. . .' She flashed a look across at Kirsty. 'If you're not planning on leaving the valley?'

That was exactly what Kirsty had been thinking as she'd struggled for sleep. Now, though. . . Well, commitments came in different guises. She couldn't run even if she wanted to. Somehow she had to struggle through this.

'Of course I'm not.'

Anthea looked at her thoughtfully. 'So why the shadows? I didn't hear you get called out in the night.'

'I wasn't.'

'So it's love-life, Dr Maine. . .'

'Anthea!'

Anthea held up her hands. 'OK. OK. I know when I'm not wanted. Just steer clear of men, that's all I can say, my Kirsty. Men are toads, and I should know. They might be toads in princely disguise, but they're toads just the same. Mark my words.'

Toads. . .

Anthea might well be right, Kirsty thought as she set off to work. Anthea had been soured by an unhappy marriage, but still. . .

'Reid Haslett is a toad. Reid Haslett is a toad.' She whispered it over and over to herself as she worked, trying to make herself believe. It didn't help at all.

The only other thought that stayed with her during the day was Mark Blainey. Today he'd be going in to see Reid. Tonight his parents would know. . .

Know what?

She couldn't bear it. She finished her last call for the night and made her way to the hospital. She had to know.

She had to know, even if it meant seeing Reid again.

He was still there. His car was in the car-park. She walked through the hospital corridors and the same sister from the night before was on duty. 'He's in his office,' she smiled, gesturing Kirsty to go on. 'I'm sure he won't mind *you* disturbing him.'

The inference was obvious, Kirsty thought grimly. Because *you* look like his ex-wife, he won't mind *you*.

Get this over, she told herself grimly. Fast.

Reid looked up as she knocked and entered, and when he saw who it was he came around the desk to greet her.

'Can't keep away from me, my Kirsty?' He smiled and Kirsty put up both hands to ward him off.

'Reid. . .'

'Kirsty.' The way he spoke her name was an endearment. A profession of love. Dear God, if only she could believe. . .

'I wanted to know about Mark,' she said stiffly. 'That's all.'

He read the fear in her face and he reacted swiftly. 'The salt test is negative, Kirsty. I agree with you that the child isn't suffering from asthma. I'm sure it's bronchiectasis. Not too much damage at this stage, though, so the outlook's fine. It's just a matter of controlling any more infections so he doesn't get worse. The bronchus will grow and give him heaps more room to cope with the irregularities the infections have already caused.'

Kirsty's breath went out of her in a long sigh. She knew there had to be other cystic fibrosis sufferers. The little boy, though. . . He had reminded her so much. . .

'Thank you,' she whispered.

'Thank you,' Reid told her, and tried to catch her hands.

He didn't. Kirsty twisted the doorknob and backed out into the corridor. 'That's all I came for, Reid. . . Dr Haslett. I'll go. . .'

'Hello, Dr Maine!' It was a woman's voice on a soft exclamation of pleasure, and Kirsty wheeled round to face Mary Harsham. Tom's wife. She had her children in tow and had obviously come in to see her husband.

'Hi, Mrs Harsham.' Kirsty smiled, relieved at the interruption. She touched Benjamin's snowy head. 'No more ticks?'

'No more ticks.' The child smiled shyly. 'And Blacky's better too.'

'Mary?' It was Tom's voice. He was clearly just inside the next door. There was a spasm of weak coughing and then the voice again. 'Benjamin, is that you?'

Mary turned inside the door, signalling that she'd like Kirsty to follow. 'It's us, dear.' She smiled, bending to kiss her ailing husband. 'And here's Dr Maine. . .'

'Bloody doctors,' Tom Harsham growled. Kirsty was standing at the ward door now, and Reid had come up behind her. 'They can't do a bloody thing. They can't fix me.'

'Tom. . .' Mary expostulated, but Reid shook his head.

'Tom's right, Mrs Harsham,' he said. 'We're having trouble shifting the pneumonia.' Reid crossed to pick up the chart. He frowned when he saw what was written there. 'We're going to have to change from the penicillin. It's not touching the infection. I think I'll move you on to tetracycline. With those headaches. . . Well, I'm starting to bet you've got psittacosis.'

Psittacosis. . . Kirsty thought briefly of what she knew of the disease. It was similar to pneumonia, but was an infection carried by birds. . .

'You may well have caught that from your birds,' Kirsty said slowly, considering. 'It makes sense.'

To her amazement Tom Harsham rose off his pillows into a sitting position. 'Who the bloody hell asked you?' he demanded. His eyes flashed fury. 'You keep your nose out of my bloody affairs. I don't keep birds. I never have, and anyone who says so is a bloody liar. So you can shove that where it hurts most, Dr bloody Maine. And get out of my room. . . Now!'

'Tom!' Reid's voice snapped across the room, but Kirsty put up a hand placatingly.

'Tom's right,' she said softly. 'I shouldn't be here. Goodnight Tom. I hope you're feeling better soon.' And she eased herself thankfully out of the door. Reid made to follow her, but a fresh paroxysm of coughing hit his patient. Reid hesitated, and Kirsty made her escape.

Whew. . . What on earth was eating Tom Harsham?

Not for the first time did she thank heaven she didn't have patients who could be rude to her. Owners were bad enough, but to treat a man who openly abused his doctor. . .

Maybe he didn't abuse Reid. Maybe it was just her. But why?

She thought about Tom Harsham as she slid into her car. Why?

The man was afraid. It hit Kirsty suddenly that behind the anger she'd seen fear in Tom Harsham's eyes.

Fear. . .

There had to be a reason. She thought back to why she had believed Tom kept birds. She hadn't imagined it. She'd heard birds in Tom's shed, and the shed hadn't been an ordinary aviary.

Suppose. . . Suppose they weren't pet birds. Suppose they were wild birds—illegally caught. That would explain their crashing hopelessly about the shed. Not pet birds disturbed, but wild birds unused to captivity. Wild birds would be much more likely carriers of psittacosis.

The first time she had seen Tom Harsham he had been carrying nets. . .

Kirsty's fingers clenched angrily into her palms. So that was how Tom Harsham supported his family! The illegal capture and sale of Australian native birds was a lucrative business. Lucrative and cruel.

Kirsty had been one of a group of vet students called in to help Australian Customs when cartons of parrots packed for transportation overseas were discovered before their flight. Each bird had been drugged and

packed inside a tiny cardboard tube. Less than half
were able to be resuscitated and released into the bush.
The dead ones were considered expendable by the
bird-dealer, she knew. If the dealer had managed to
place a quarter of the birds on to the overseas market
he'd have made a fortune.

You're not sure. Kirsty told herself. She thought of
Mary Harsham's tired face and grimaced. You need
evidence, Kirsty, before you go getting the Harshams
into trouble. The only evidence now is hearing birds
Tom says don't exist, and seeing Tom come out of the
bush carrying nets. Hardly enough to convict the man.

Still. . .

She drove to her surgery, thinking hard, and finally
rang the local Fisheries and Wildlife officer. She
couldn't act on her own. Len Hart was a big, amiable
man, who she knew would act with sense.

'You could well be right,' he told her. 'Glossy black
and sulphur-crested cockatoos have been appearing on
the market over the last six months, and we know the
dealers have to have a source around here.'

'I've no evidence.'

'I'll get a warrant. The magistrate will give me one
on the basis of what you've told me.'

'Len?'

'Yes.'

'The whole family is at the hospital now. I'm still
treating their dog. I could just go. . .'

'And have a quiet look around.' Len grunted in
satisfaction. 'It'd cause much less trouble.' Like Kirsty,
he knew the serving of a warrant would stir up local
gossip. 'Yeah, OK. I'll meet you there. If you're checking on the dog I could be just keeping you company.'

'You know the Harshams'?'

'I know the Harshams'.'

Len wasn't there when Kirsty reached the place. The
house was in darkness, but as Kirsty's car stopped a
dark shape launched itself out of nowhere, barking

viciously. Blacky made a great watchdog.

'It's OK, Blacky.' Kirsty knelt on the dew-wet grass and made her peace with the dog. 'It's only me.' She flicked on the torch in her hand. 'Want to show me round?'

Of course he did. The dog responded to the affection in her tone with a delighted wag and strutted of towards the sheds, as if he knew what she wanted to see.

There was no frantic fluttering this time. The birds, it seemed, were gone. Kirsty pressed on the doorhandle, expecting it to be locked, but it swung open beneath her hand.

There were no adult birds, but evidence of their stay was everywhere. There were cages, and recent droppings. There were bright feathers, and traces of blood where birds had crashed themselves against the bars.

It wasn't enough. If the birds were gone, they'd never get a conviction.

And then a faint chirping started in the corner, and the chirping set off more. Feathers rustled and birds stirred on their perches in a row of cages at the end of the shed. Kirsty's torch swept over them and she swore under her breath.

Spoon-feeders. . . The cages were full of fledglings. These little birds had been collected while still in their nests. Their incubation had been done by the parent birds but once they were old enough to feed from a spoon they'd been stolen from the nest and brought here.

The baby birds had been roused now from their repose and wanted something for their pains. Food. . . The half-grown fledglings squawked indignantly as the torch beam landed on them. So where was supper?

It was a real industry. Kirsty walked from cage to cage, looking at the species represented. The cockatoos were mostly glossy blacks, their distinctive red tail feathers just starting to develop. Her sympathy for

Mary Harsham was fading by the minute. She must be helping her husband in an operation this big.

Why had he been netting wild birds if he had so many fledglings? Spoon-feeders were much easier birds to handle than wild adults. He must have had an urgent order, Kirsty thought, knowing the methods used to catch wild birds. He'd have drugged seed, then rigged a box net to fall down over them.

And then a beam of torchlight came in through the door. Kirsty turned thankfully towards it. 'Len?'

It wasn't Len. It was Tom Harsham.

Tom stood, his hand holding the doorknob to steady himself. His face was soaked in sweat. Obviously he'd made a huge effort to get himself out of bed.

'I knew you'd come here,' he growled. 'Stupid, interfering bitch. . .'

'You should be in hospital,' Kirsty said unsteadily. 'Tom, you're sick.'

'Not as sick as you're going to be.'

He raised his hand from the door. Blue metal glinted in the torchlight and a shotgun pointed straight at Kirsty.

A shotgun. . .

Kirsty's first thought, stupidly, was that it would be a shotgun! A rifle in those unsteady hands would have missed. A shotgun, though. . . At this range he couldn't miss as it sprayed pellets toward her.

'Don't be stupid,' she said unsteadily. 'For heaven's sake, Tom. At the moment the charge is illegal keeping of wildlife. Do you want to change that to murder?'

He was beyond listening to reason. His illness must be making him almost delirious, Kirsty thought desperately.

'Tom. . .'

His finger tightened on the trigger.

'Tom!' The shout came from outside the shed. Tom moved instinctively inside and swung around to face the voice. 'Tom! For God's sake man, don't do anything stupid. Tom. . .'

Reid. . . It was Reid. She'd recognise that voice anywhere.

'Tom. . .' Reid was yelling as he ran, his torch-beam cutting through the night. And Tom Harsham lifted his gun and aimed straight along the torch-beam. Reid first, it seemed, and Kirsty second.

Kirsty first. She launched herself straight across the shed like a wildcat. Her hands caught the gun and pushed it up.

Tom swore and shoved, but Kirsty was fighting for her life. Fighting for Reid's life. Her fingers clung to the barrel as he hauled it back. . .back. . .

And his fingers clenched on the trigger. The blast exploded into the night and the night disappeared.

CHAPTER TWELVE

'KIRSTY. . .'

There was someone calling her name. There was some reason why she had to wake.

Kirsty lay on her pillows and considered. For some reason it seemed extraordinarily hard to open her eyes. They were heavy. Her head was aching. Why bother?

'Kirsty! Kirsty, love. . .'

She knew why she had to bother. It was Reid calling her name. The hands holding hers, urging her to wakefulness, imparting strength with his touch, were Reid's.

Reid. . . Her love.

Her eyelids fluttered. She flinched from the light and let them fall, and then she tried again.

'Kirsty!'

The voice had changed. The desperate hopelessness was lifting. Not much. Reid was hardly allowing himself to hope.

'Come on, Kirsty, love. Open your eyes. Oh, God, Kirsty, you have to open your eyes. My Kirsty. . . My love. . .'

The corners of Kirsty's mouth curved upward in the beginnings of a smile. She thought of the words she wanted to say. Could she? It seemed extraordinarily hard to make her lips move.

'That's hardly a professional approach, Doctor,' Kirsty whispered, and opened her eyes.

She was in hospital. It was day. The sun's early rays were lying over her coverlet. The blind had been adjusted so that it wasn't at full strength but even that hurt. She put her hand to her head but Reid was before her, his fingers holding hers as she touched the dressing.

'Welcome back, my Kirsty.' Reid's voice sounded as though it was full of joy. And full of tears. . .

Tears. . .

Tears for her. . .

She looked wonderingly up at him and the rough skin of his cheeks was wet. He was smiling, though, and his smile told her more than she could ever be told in words. His smile told her that he had been through hell. . . For her. . .

'Reid. . .'

'Don't try to move.' His voice was unsteady. His hand touched her face. 'You've given us a hell of a fright. . .'

'Us?' Her voice was so darned weak. It was as though someone else was talking, from a long, long way away.

'Me, in particular.' Reid smiled. 'But there's also a fair crowd in the waiting-room who are desperate to know you've decided to live.' His voice broke suddenly and he bent his head to kiss her. 'My lovely, foolish, brave and wondrous Kirsty. Of all the stupid, stupid things. . .'

'He was going to shoot you. . .'

'So you put yourself between the gun and me. Very sensible.' Still his voice was unsteady.

She made her hand move once more to the dressing. 'So. . .so he shot me?'

'You were bloody lucky.' Reid's hand covered hers, stilling her inquisitive fingers. 'The bulk of the shot pellets missed you. You were so darned close they didn't have a chance to spread. A couple seared across the side of your head, though, Kirsty. You have a nasty gash, and a few stitches.'

'Oh. . .'

'Your hair will grow back,' Reid told her softly. 'No permanent scarring. . .' He took a deep breath. 'We weren't sure, though. You wouldn't regain consciousness. I took X-rays, but couldn't see any damage. There must have been some, though, to knock you out for nearly twelve hours. There's a plane on its way now to airlift you to Melbourne.'

'I don't want to go.' Kirsty's eyes widened and her voice gathered strength. This was important. 'I don't——'

'Why not, my Kirsty?'

Kirsty looked up at him. It must be so obvious why not. So obvious. . . She put out a finger and touched him, as though afraid he was a shadow.

'Sister. . .' Reid called for the nurse, but his eyes didn't leave Kirsty.

'Dr Haslett?' A nurse appeared from the doorway as though she had been waiting. She smiled down at Kirsty and relief flashed into her eyes. 'Oh, thank goodness. . .'

'Sister, could you inform the people in the waiting-room—Mrs Watts and her daughter, Mr Henderson. . .?'

'And Mrs Henderson and the Blaineys and half the town.' The nurse smiled. 'Not to mention three dogs and two cats, which I've ordered to wait in the car-park.'

'Whoever. Could you tell them that Dr Maine shows every sign of recovering. And, Sister. . .?'

'Yes?'

'In the bottom of the filing cabinet in my office there's a framed photo of my ex-wife. Could you bring it here, please?'

'Certainly, Doctor.' The nurse was puzzled but obedient. She glanced from Reid to Kirsty and left them. A minute later she reappeared, bearing the photograph. 'Is this what you wanted, Doctor?'

'Yes.' Reid held it up to the nurse. 'Sister, in your opinion, does this photograph resemble in any way the woman in this bed?'

The nurse frowned. She looked from the photograph to Kirsty and back again. 'Of course not.'

'Thank you, Sister,' Reid said dismissively. Then, as the nurse disappeared, he lifted a mirror from the wall and held it for Kirsty to see. 'What do you think, Kirsty?'

Kirsty blinked. The image in the mirror was not her. Her glossy black curls had been cut short to let them access her wounded head better. What curls there were were still caked in dried blood. One side of her face was heavily bandaged and her eyes were dark with shadow. She looked at the photograph of Stephanie and tried to smile.

'I guess. . .I guess I don't.'

'Good.' Reid bent and placed the photograph in the rubbish bin. 'That's where that belongs, my Kirsty.' He took her hands in his. 'The photographs you have of Neil don't belong there, though, Kirsty. Neil has a place in our lives. He's still a part of us, and his photographs will be honoured as part of you. If Neil helped make you what you are today then I'm eternally grateful to him. I have no wish to replace him.'

'Reid——'

'But I do want to marry you, my Kirsty. I swear my love has nothing to do with what you once looked like. I swear it has nothing to do with what Stephanie once looked like.' He raised three fingers in a boy scout's salute. 'Scout's honour.' He smiled.

'Doctor's honour. . .' Kirsty smiled weakly back at him. 'Oh, Reid. . .'

'I know.' He was running his finger lightly down her cheek in a gesture of absolute love. 'You're so damned weak. I shouldn't demand a commitment at a time like this. The thing is. . .I might never have you so weak again. Please, God, may I never be so frightened again in my life. But I'm not a man to miss opportunities. So just say, Yes, thank you, Dr Haslett, I'll marry you, and I'll let you drift nicely off to sleep.'

'Reid——'

His hands held hers. 'Please, my Kirsty.'

The voice wasn't insistent. It was a plea, and there was love and hope and despair all mixed up in it.

And Kirsty knew that it was all for her.

'Yes, thank you, Dr Reid. . .' Kirsty whispered. 'I'll marry you. . .'

And she did what the doctor ordered.

She drifted off to sleep.

CHAPTER THIRTEEN

A QUIET wedding wasn't an option in Woongarra. Most of the valley were present when on a calm spring day, with the air full of promise of life to come, the valley's two doctors became one.

Eve was bridesmaid in glorious pink.

'I can't have bridesmaids,' Kirsty had protested, laughing. 'It's my second wedding. A quiet wedding!' But Eve's smile had slipped, and Kirsty had shaken her head and helped her choose a dress almost as sumptuous as her own.

The valley had taken over. 'No wedding-dress?' Irene Henderson had thrown up her hands in horror. 'Leave it to me.' And the vision of silk and satin was the most beautiful dress Kirsty had ever seen. In deference to Kirsty's widowhood Irene had embroidered tiny gold roses around the neck and hemline, but otherwise it was virgin-white.

'A proper bride,' Irene said in satisfaction as Kirsty tried it on. 'Oh, my dear. . . You are so beautiful!'

A simple journey to church?

Bob Henderson borrowed an ancient coach. The stable-lads scrubbed it until it shone, and helped Margaret Haslett school Misty and Miles to pull the carriage. The horses' manes and tails were plaited with white satin and they held their heads high.

A quiet wedding-breakfast?

'Not if the Returned Soldiers' League's got anything to do with it,' Bert Freeman growled, and the meal was amazing. The town's women had formed a committee to make the cake, and they were so proud. . . Well, they had to come. The whole town had to come.

And in the end Reid and Kirsty hardly noticed. All they noticed as they made their pledges was each other, but the atmosphere of peace and love around them was a further pledge of their own love.

They had gifts from everywhere. But one. . . One stood apart from all the rest. A coincidental gift. . .

The day drew to a close. They had married in the morning and the reception—the huge party which the entire valley deemed it their right to attend—would go on until the next morning, but as the sun dropped low in the sky Reid carried his laughing, lovely bride through the throng and placed her tenderly in the waiting car. Kirsty sank back in a cloud of white silk and waved to the people she was leaving.

They were leaving for a short while, with the health of the valley's people and animals trusted to two locums. Two weeks somewhere no one would ever find them, Reid had promised. Kirsty didn't know where and she didn't want to. It was enough. . .

But first their gift. . .

Len Hart, the Fisheries and Wildlife officer, was waiting where he had promised. He'd rung Kirsty the day before and told her what was happening tonight.

'But it's the day we're getting married,' Kirsty had exclaimed, and then paused. 'Oh. . .'

Len had planned it. She knew. . .

Kirsty had only been to this place once before. She'd been here the night she had met Tom Harsham coming out of the bush with his nets over his arms.

Reid drew to a halt as Len was pulling crates from the back of a truck, placing each crate with care on the grass verge. He grinned at the pair of them— Reid immaculate in his morning suit and Kirsty in her floating white cloud of a bridal gown.

'Well, well.' He grinned. 'A pair of workers if ever I saw them.' His smile broadened. 'Congratulations to the pair of you.'

'On behalf of my wife and I——' Reid began ponderously, and Kirsty poked him in the ribs and chuckled.

'Very wifely,' Reid retorted, hugging her close while

his laughing eyes promised retribution. Soon. . .

'I thought you'd like to be in on this,' Len told them. 'The court case is over. The birds have been carefully acclimatised. It's time to put them back where they came from.'

'The court case. . .' Kirsty's mist of happiness evaporated for a moment. She had given evidence the week before but it had now been finalised. 'What. . .? What happened?'

'They gave Tom a hefty fine and a suspended sentence,' Reid told her. 'Glossy black Cockatoos aren't on the endangered list, so the penalty's not as stiff as it might have been. The entrapment of the birds was his first offence. And as for shooting you—psittacosis causes delirium as a side effect. He wasn't in his right mind, Kirsty. He walked out of hospital in his pyjamas and forced his wife to give him the car keys. He's damned lucky he didn't kill himself on the way.'

'Do you want to help with this?' Len demanded, still smiling. 'I'd like to get home to my dinner. I suppose you two can think of nothing better than to stand by the road and gossip. . .'

Reid grinned. 'I can think of one or two things,' he confessed. His arm tightened around his bride. 'But this is Kirsty's job. . .'

'You'll stand back and let a woman work?' Len grinned, and Kirsty leaned down in her bridal white, unclipped the first cage door and lifted the hatch.

Five black cockatoos emerged warily from the box. They hopped out on to the grass, sat for less than a second, and then launched themselves straight for the setting sun.

Kirsty moved from box to box. Her heart was swirling in happiness, and behind her the two men watched. She could feel their satisfaction. She could feel Reid's love. . .

And then the last of the birds took off into the night sky. Len gathered his cages and bade them farewell.

'I'm off to my dinner,' he said, but Kirsty and Reid

hardly heard him. They were staring after the black
shadows in the sky. They were staring at freedom.

And then Kirsty turned her face up to Reid.
Freedom. . . It had many different guises, but here,
then, was hers.

She was free. She was one.

She was whole again.

Reid bent to kiss her, and Kirsty Maine. . .Kirsty
Haslett. . .could ask no more.

MILLS & BOON

Kids & Kisses—where kids and romance go hand in hand.

This summer Mills & Boon brings you Kids & Kisses— a set
of titles featuring lovable kids as the stars of the show!

Look out for
Fire Beneath the Ice by Helen Brooks
in August 1995

Kids…one of life's joys, one of life's treasures.

Kisses…of warmth, kisses of passion, kisses from mothers
and kisses from lovers.

In Kids & Kisses…every story has it all.

*Available from W.H. Smith, John Menzies, Volume One, Forbuoys,
Martins, Woolworths, Tesco, Asda, Safeway and other paperback stockists.*

MILLS & BOON

are proud to present...

A set of warm, involving romances in which you can meet
some fascinating members of our heroes' and heroines'
families. Published each month in the Romance series.

Look out for "Make-Believe Family" by Elizabeth Duke
in August 1995.

Family Ties: Romances that take the family to heart.

Available from WH Smith, John Menzies, Volume One, Forbuoys, Martins,
Woolworths, Tesco, Asda, Safeway and other paperback stockists.

MILLS & BOON

Relive the romance with our great new series…

Bestselling romances brought back to you by popular demand

Each month we will be bringing you two books in one volume from the best of the best. So if you missed a favourite Romance the first time around, here is your chance to relive the magic from some of our most popular authors.

We know you'll love our first By Request volume— two complete novels by bestselling author **Penny Jordan—*Game of Love* and *Time for Trust*.**

Available: August 1995   Price: £3.99

Available from WH Smith, John Menzies, Volume One, Forbuoys, Martins, Woolworths, Tesco, Asda, Safeway and other paperback stockists.

Return this coupon and we'll send you 4 Love on Call novels and a mystery gift absolutely FREE! We'll even pay the postage and packing for you.

We're making you this offer to introduce you to the benefits of Reader Service: FREE home delivery of brand-new Love on Call novels, at least a month before they are available in the shops, FREE gifts and a monthly Newsletter packed with information.

Accepting these FREE books and gift places you under no obligation to buy, you may cancel at any time, even after receiving just your free shipment. Simply complete the coupon below and send it to:

HARLEQUIN MILLS & BOON, FREEPOST, PO BOX 70, CROYDON, CR9 9EL.

No stamp needed

Yes, please send me 4 free Love on Call novels and a mystery gift. I understand that unless you hear from me, I will receive 4 superb new titles every month for just £1.99* each postage and packing free. I am under no obligation to purchase any books and I may cancel or suspend my subscription at any time, but the free books and gifts will be mine to keep in any case. (I am over 18 years of age)

2EP5D

Ms/Mrs/Miss/Mr _____

Address _____

_____

_____ Postcode _____

Offer closes 31st January 1996. We reserve the right to refuse an application. *Prices and terms subject to change without notice. Offer only valid in UK and Ireland and is not available to current subscribers to this series. **Readers in Ireland please write to: P.O. Box 4546, Dublin 24.** Overseas readers please write for details.

You may be mailed with offers from other reputable companies as a result of this application. Please tick box if you would prefer not to receive such offers.

mps MAILING PREFERENCE SERVICE

DMA

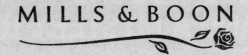

MILLS & BOON

LOVE CALL

The books for enjoyment this month are:

LOVE WITHOUT MEASURE	Caroline Anderson
VERSATILE VET	Mary Bowring
TARRANT'S PRACTICE	Abigail Gordon
DOCTOR'S HONOUR	Marion Lennox

Treats in store!

Watch next month for the following absorbing stories:

MIDWIFE'S DILEMMA	Lilian Darcy
MADE FOR EACH OTHER	Elizabeth Harrison
HOSPITAL AT RISK	Clare Lavenham
SEEING EYE TO EYE	Josie Metcalfe

Available from W.H. Smith, John Menzies, Volume One, Forbuoys,
Martins, Tesco, Asda, Safeway and other paperback stockists.

Readers in South Africa - write to:
IBS, Private Bag X3010, Randburg 2125.